"Marriage is a serious affair."

The Professor paused before continuing, "And it occurred to me that I may have been overhasty in broaching the subject. Nevertheless, I hope that you have given it your consideration. Perhaps, though, you have a boyfriend of your own—or you may not wish to marry."

His voice was quiet and very faintly accented.

"Me? A boyfriend? Heavens, no. At least—" Trixie hesitated "—not since I started my training."

"You have no objections to being married, do you?"

"None at all," she told him soberly, and thought what a strange conversation they were having.

"So you will consider becoming my wife? But perhaps I am too old?"

"Pooh," she said. "Age hasn't anything to do with it." And it was at that moment, looking up into his concerned face, that Trixie fell in love.

Betty Neels is well-known for her romances set in the Netherlands, which is hardly surprising. She married a Dutchman and spent the first twelve years of their marriage living in Holland and working as a nurse. Today, she and her husband make their home in an ancient stone cottage in England's West Country, but they return to Holland often. She loves to explore tiny villages and tour privately owned homes there in order to lend an air of authenticity to the background of her books.

Books by Betty Neels

HARLEQUIN ROMANCE

AN UNLIKELY ROMANCE
Betty Neels

Harlequin Books

TORONTO • NEW YORK • LONDON
AMSTERDAM • PARIS • SYDNEY • HAMBURG
STOCKHOLM • ATHENS • TOKYO • MILAN
MADRID • WARSAW • BUDAPEST • AUCKLAND

Original hardcover edition published in 1992
by Mills & Boon Limited

ISBN 0-373-03222-6

Harlequin Romance first edition September 1992

AN UNLIKELY ROMANCE

Copyright © 1992 by Betty Neels.

Printed in U.S.A.

CHAPTER ONE

TRIXIE DOVETON, trundling old Mrs Crowe from the bathroom back to her ward, allowed a small, almost soundless sigh to escape her lips. The ward doors had been thrust open and Professor van der Brink-Schaaksma was coming unhurriedly towards her. He had a sheaf of papers under one arm and a book, one finger marking his place, in his other hand. He wasn't due for another twenty minutes and Sister Snell was already hurrying after him, intent on heading him off with a cup of coffee in her office while her nurses raced around getting the patients into the correct state of readiness. He was always doing it, reflected Trixie, rolling Mrs Crowe's ample person into her bed; arriving early, not arriving at all, or arriving half an hour late, tendering the politest of apologies when he discovered his mistake, his brilliant mind engrossed in some ticklish problem concerning endocrinology, a science of which he was a leading exponent. Trixie took another look at him while she tucked Mrs Crowe into her blankets; he was such a nice man— the nicest she had ever met, not that she had actually met him, only seen him from time to time on the ward or in one of the corridors, either with his nose buried in some book or other or surrounded by students. She was quite sure that he wasn't even aware that she existed. He was towering over Sister Snell now, smiling gently down at her rather cross face, a tall, very large man, his pale hair grey at the temples, his eyes heavy-lidded and, she suspected, quite unaware of his good looks. He

5

glanced up and she glanced away quickly, and when she peeped again it was to see his massive back disappearing through the doors.

'He's a nice chap, ain't he?' observed Mrs Crowe. 'No side to him neither.'

She beamed at Trixie's face; she was a friendly girl who would always find time to say a few words, offer sympathy when needed and even, when her seniors weren't looking, put in a few curlers for such of her patients who needed to be smartened up for visitors. She would have enlarged upon this but Staff Nurse Bennett, racing up and down like a demented sergeant major, had come to a halt by the bed.

'Nurse Doveton, for heaven's sake get a move on. Professor van der Brink-Schaaksma's here, far too soon of course, and the place is like a pigsty and you standing there gossiping. It's time you learned to be quicker; you'll never make a good nurse at this rate. All this mooning about...'

She hurried away, saying over her shoulder, 'Find Nurse Saunders, she's in one of the treatment-rooms, and tell her to make sure all the path lab reports are on the trolley.'

Trixie patted Mrs Crowe's plump shoulder and trotted off obediently. She was a small girl, nicely plump with a face which, while not plain, was hardly pretty; her nose was too short and her mouth too large, but it curved up at the corners and her smile was charming. Only her eyes were beautiful, large and hazel with pale brown lashes to match the neat head of hair under her cap. She was twenty-three years old, an orphan and prepared to make the best of it. She had the kindest of hearts, a romantic nature and a good deal of common sense, and she liked her job. In another year she would have completed her training, despite Staff Nurse Bennett's gloomy prediction. She was aware that she would never be another Florence Nightingale, but at least she would be earning her living.

Nurse Saunders was in a bad mood; she had had words with her boyfriend on the previous evening and had no chance of seeing him for several days to come. She listened to Trixie's message impatiently, thumped down the tray of instruments she was holding and said, 'Oh, all right. Just put these away for me and look sharp about it. Why can't the man come when he's supposed to?'

She didn't give Trixie a chance to answer, but went into the ward, slamming the door behind her.

Trixie arranged the instruments tidily in the cupboard, tidied up a tiny bit and opened the door; the professor wouldn't have finished his coffee yet. She would have time to slip into the sluice-room and find something to do there. The coffee must have been tepid or the professor's mouth made of cast iron, for he was there, in the ward, only a few yards away, deep in talk with Dr Johnson, while Sister hovered at his other side against a reverent background of medical students, and behind them the furious face of Staff Nurse Bennett. Trixie, intent on a prudent retreat into the treatment-room, took a step backwards, tripped over her own feet and tumbled untidily to the floor. She had barely touched it when the professor paused in the discussion, stooped forward, plucked her back on to the offending feet, dusted her down, patted her on her shoulder without apparently having looked at her and resumed his conversation. It had all happened so quickly that beyond a startled look from Sister and grins from the students the unfortunate incident might never have been. Trixie, edging her way to a discreet distance, doubted if the professor had noticed her; he was notoriously absent-minded, and he would have done the same thing for a child, an old lady or an overturned chair.

In the fastness of the sluice-room she polished and scrubbed everything in sight; it wasn't her job but she felt that she should make amends for annoying Staff Nurse Bennett, and—once that young lady had had the chance to tell her—Sister.

Sure enough, later that morning she was told to go to Sister's office where she was reprimanded by that lady. 'Professor van der Brink-Schaaksma is not to be bothered in such a manner, Nurse Doveton. He has far more important things to do than picking up girls off the floor. How could you be so clumsy?'

'I was surprised,' observed Trixie reasonably, 'and he need not have picked me up—I mean I didn't ask for help or anything like that.' She smiled kindly at her senior, who was quite scarlet with ill temper. 'I'm so sorry if it upset you, Sister. It was most tiresome of me but I don't think the professor noticed anything.'

Sister Snell said crossly, 'It is to be hoped not. Go and do Mrs Watts's ulcer and then take her down to physiotherapy. When are you off duty?'

'Five o'clock, Sister, and then I have a day off.'

The day with its manifold tasks wore on. Because Mrs Watts had held things up by feeling sick, Trixie was late for her midday dinner. The canteen was almost empty by the time she got there, although several of her friends were still sitting over their cups of tea. She fetched boiled cod—it was Friday—and mashed potatoes and parsnips, and joined them.

'You're late,' observed Mary Fitzjohn accusingly. She was a girl who took pride in plain speaking, correcting people and telling them if they had a ladder in their tights or their caps were on crooked. She had a good opinion of herself and was tolerated in an amused way.

Trixie lavished tomato sauce on the fish. 'Mrs Watts felt sick.' She began to gobble her dinner. 'I must go over to my room and pack a bag. I've got a day off.'

'Going home?' a fat girl with a pretty face asked.

'Yes. It's Margaret's birthday.'

'A party?'

'Well, a cocktail party.'

'What will you wear?' chorused several voices.

'There's the blue crêpe or that brown velvet. The brown, I think—after all, it is October.'

'Surely you should have something new and smart for a cocktail party?' asked Mary, looking down her nose.

'Me? I shan't know anyone there—Margaret has masses of friends, you know, and I don't know any of them. I mean I don't intend to dazzle them—it's her party...'

'I should have thought——' began Mary, and was silenced by a general chorus of 'shut up'. Trixie dealt with treacle tart, swallowed her tea and darted off; there was still ten minutes before she needed to be back on duty and in her room she packed an overnight bag with neat efficiency, straightened her cap and made her way from the nurses' home to the ward once more. She wasn't really looking forward to the party; she had lived with Aunt Alice and Uncle William ever since her parents had died in an accident when she was ten years old, and although they had educated her, fed her and clothed her and in their way been kind to her, she had never been quite happy, for somehow the knowledge that they were doing their duty and at the same time resenting her being there had been borne in upon her before very long. As she had grown she had realised that their interest was centred on their daughter Margaret, pretty and popular and spoilt, and as soon as she had left school Trixie had suggested that she should train for a nurse, but to her surprise this was frowned upon. Margaret had no intention of doing anything and Aunt Alice had realised that if Trixie were allowed to leave home there might be raised eyebrows over the fact that, while her own daughter stayed at home enjoying herself, their ward had to earn her own living. So Trixie had spent several years making herself useful around the large house at Highgate, meeting very few people, for Aunt Alice had let it be known that she was a shy girl and disliked social occasions, and she might have been there still if one of Margaret's more eligible men friends hadn't started to show an interest in Trixie, and, since she hadn't liked him very much and gave him no encouragement, he'd begun to feel himself quite interested and serious about her. It was time, decided Aunt Alice, to do something about the matter. Trixie had been told that, now that she was older and with no prospect of marriage in sight, if she still wished to do so she might apply for training at one of the London teaching hospitals. Something she'd done very quickly before anyone could change their minds. She wasn't quite twenty-one when she began her training, which from Aunt Alice's point of view was very convenient, for there was no opportunity to celebrate the occasion. Trixie was given a gold watch and lunch at the Ritz on her day off and told to go to Highgate whenever she wished. 'For your room will always be ready for you, Trixie,' said her aunt. 'We shall miss you; you have been like a second daughter to us.'

Somehow the remark had sounded final.

She didn't get off duty very punctually; she wasn't a clock-watcher and the patients knew that, so that she was always the one to fill last-minute water jugs, find lost spectacles and exchange someone's magazine with someone else's. She changed quickly, caught up her overnight bag and hurried to catch a bus to Highgate. The bus queue was long and impatient and by the time she got to Highgate it was almost seven o'clock. Her uncle and aunt dined at eight o'clock and she had been warned that there were to be guests. She arrived hot and tired to be greeted with barely concealed impatience by her aunt.

'Really, Trixie, you might at least try to be punctual for once. This is Margaret's birthday celebration, after all. Tomorrow I shall want you to arrange the flowers for the party, you do them so well...'

Trixie went up to the second-floor room, which, as Aunt Alice had pointed out, reasonably enough, would do very well for her now that she came home so seldom, and got into the brown velvet, did her face and her hair and slipped into the drawing-room just as the first guests were arriving.

The dinner party was really for their old friends, Margaret's godparents and a sprinkling of aunts and uncles, none of whom would have enjoyed her birthday party but who would have been hurt if uninvited.

Trixie, between two elderly gentlemen, brothers of Aunt Alice, ate her dinner and made dinner-table conversation, something she did very nicely, so that they remarked upon her quiet charm to Aunt Alice later that evening.

'Nice girl,' said one of them. 'Can't think why she hasn't been snapped up. Make a splendid wife.'

'Very shy and withdrawn and engrossed in her nursing,' Aunt Alice observed with a snap. 'Of course, dear Margaret is quite different...'

Trixie was busy the next day; there were flowers to arrange, the telephone to answer and help to give to her aunt's cook and housemaid, and later the bits and pieces to unpack and arrange from the caterers.

Margaret wandered in and out, unpacking her presents and leaving a trail of paper behind her, pleased with herself and everyone else. She had thanked Trixie for the silk scarf she had been given, asked in a casually friendly fashion about her work and wandered away again without waiting for a reply. Although they were cousins and brought up together and, for that matter, got on well, Margaret had always adopted a slightly condescending manner towards Trixie—the poor relation, presentable enough and a pleasant companion when there was no one else around, and now quite rightly earning her own living. From time to time Margaret took her out to lunch or to the cinema and went home feeling that she had done her duty and been kind to her cousin.

Dressed in the brown velvet, Trixie took a look at herself in the looking-glass inside the old-fashioned wardrobe. Her reflection didn't please her. The dress was well made, nicely cut and fitted her person well, but there was nothing about it to attract a second glance. She wished that she had Margaret's glorious fair hair, cascading around her pretty face in a riot of curls, but her own pale brown hair was fine and straight and long and she had always worn it in a chignon so that its beauty was quite hidden. She put a final dab of powder on her nose and went downstairs.

Margaret had any number of friends. The big drawing-room was soon crowded, and Trixie sipped sherry and went around greeting the people she knew, young men and women she had known since her school days, but the majority of those there were unknown to her, smart and noisy, ignoring the other guests.

Presently she came face to face with Margaret, who caught her by the arm. 'Hello—isn't this fun? I say, Mother's just had a phone call from Colonel Vosper—he was invited to dinner yesterday and had to refuse, now he's phoned to say he'll come for half an hour just to wish me many happy returns. He's bringing a stuffy professor with him—they're going to some dinner or other! This isn't quite their scene, is it?'

'If they're going to a dinner,' said Trixie matter-of-factly, 'they won't stay long, will they? Aunt Alice has gone to the door. It must be the colonel; shouldn't you be there too?'

'I suppose so.' She paused to look Trixie over. 'That's a pretty awful dress you're wearing—brown doesn't suit you, you look like a church mouse.' She added, casually kind, 'You'd look nice in green or blue—you ought to get yourself some pretty clothes.'

She drifted away, a sight to gladden the eyes in her golden sequinned jacket and layered silk skirt. Trixie watched her progress through the crowded room, but not enviously, for she hadn't an envious nature, only wondering if a sequinned jacket would do for her own person what brown velvet quite obviously could not.

There was a little bustle at the door as the colonel came in; an elderly man, still upright and handsome. His companion followed him in and paused to talk to Aunt Alice and then Margaret, so that Trixie had ample time to study Professor van der Brink-Schaaksma, immaculately handsome in black tie.

She gave a little gasp of surprise and retired prudently behind a group of people, from where she surveyed his progress through the room with Margaret. Her cousin was exerting her charm, a pretty hand on his arm, looking up into his face in open admiration. He was so completely out of his element, thought Trixie. He had put every other man in the room in the shade, but he was unaware of it; indeed, although he was smiling down at her cousin, listening to her chatter, she had the strong impression that he was probably contemplating some tricky aspect of endocrinology. She had seen that absorbed look on his face often enough to recognise it.

She had moved back even further, intent on keeping out of his line of vision, and it was unfortunate that her aunt should call her by name in her rather loud voice.

'Trixie,' cooed Aunt Alice, *fortissimo*, 'come here, dear, the colonel wants to see you.'

There was nothing for it but to abandon her dark corner and make her way across the room to where the old gentleman stood, and of course at that same moment Margaret and the professor had paused to speak to someone and had turned round to watch her. She was unable to avoid his glance, but she gave no sign of recognition, and, to her great feeling of relief, nor did he.

Well, why should he? He had never actually looked at her on the ward and she was dressed differently. She retired to a sofa with the colonel for the kind of chat her companion enjoyed; he was holding forth about politics, modern youth and modern warfare to a listening audience. Trixie was a very good listener. He got up to go presently. 'A nice little talk, my dear; I wish we could have stayed longer but we must attend a function, as you may know.' He looked around him. 'Where is Krijn? Ah—with Margaret. Such a very pretty girl, even an absent-minded professor may be forgiven if he falls under her spell.'

He patted Trixie's shoulder. 'We must talk again,' he told her as they said goodbye.

She slipped away to the other end of the room, reluctant to come face to face with the professor, and presently the guests began to leave. A small party of Margaret's closest friends were taking her out to dinner and Trixie was kept busy finding coats and wraps.

'Coming with us?' asked one of the girls.

There was no need for her to reply. Margaret had overheard and said at once, 'Oh, Trixie hates going to restaurants, and besides, she's on duty at that hospital of hers at the crack of dawn.'

Neither of which was true, but Trixie said nothing. Margaret didn't mean to be unkind; she was thoughtless and spoilt and ever since they had been children together she had been accustomed to the idea that Trixie was by way of being a poor relation, to be treated as one of the family but at the same time to make herself useful and obliging.

Trixie had put up with that, for she was grateful for having a home and a family of sorts. All the same, it had been a heaven-sent blessing when the eligible young man had fancied himself in love with her and she had at last embarked on a life of her own. If she had been hurt she had very firmly never allowed anyone to see it. She saw them into their cars and went back into the house to eat her dinner with her aunt and uncle and agree, with sincerity, that Margaret was quite beautiful. 'If only she would settle down,' observed Aunt Alice. 'That was a very distinguished man who came with the colonel—a professor, too. I wonder what he does...'

Trixie, who could have told her, remained silent.

She left the house the next morning without having seen Margaret again. She was on duty at ten o'clock for the rest of the day and only her uncle had been at breakfast with her. 'I'll say goodbye to your aunt and Margaret for you,' he told her. 'They both need a good rest after all the trouble they went to for the party.' He sounded faintly reproachful. 'A pity you couldn't have had a day or two more free to give a hand.'

Trixie said yes, it was, wasn't it? and forbore from reminding him that she had been up until one o'clock that morning, helping the maid to get the room straight again. She thanked him for the party, left polite messages for Aunt Alice and Margaret and took herself off, back to the East End where Timothy's spread its forbidding grey stone, encircled by narrow busy streets and rows of poky houses. The ugly old hospital was her home now and back in her room in the nurses' home she surveyed it with all the pride of a houseowner. Over the months she had bought cushions, a table-lamp, a pretty bedspread and a picture or two. She admired them now as she got into her uniform and then went along to the tiny kitchen to make a cup of tea. Some of her friends were there and they took their mugs back to her room for the last few minutes before they had to go on duty, full of questions about the party.

'Was there anyone exciting there?' asked Mary.

'They were almost all people I didn't know.' Trixie almost mentioned the professor and decided not to; after all he was hardly exciting, although he had looked remarkably handsome... 'There was a dinner party for godmothers and godfathers and uncles and aunts,' she explained. 'The party was for Margaret's friends.'

'What were the clothes like?' someone asked.

They spent the rest of the time discussing fashion before going off to their various wards.

Ten o'clock in the morning wasn't a favourite time at which to go on duty; housemen were checking up on patients, several of whom were being taken to various departments for treatment or tests, and those who were left in their beds wanted things—hot drinks, cold drinks, pillows turned, sheets changed, bedpans, injections, two-hourly feeds... Trixie went to and fro happily enough; Staff Nurse Bennett had days off and the part-time staff nurse doing her job was married with young children, tolerant of the most troublesome patient and kind but firm with the nurses. Trixie went off duty that evening content with her day and slept the moment her head touched the pillow. With Staff Nurse Bennett still away the following day was just as satisfying. Trixie, off duty at five o'clock, joined several of her friends and went to the cinema and then gathered in the kitchen to eat the fish and chips they had bought on the way home. Life might not be very exciting, but at least it offered friendships, security and held few surprises. She slept the sleep of the hardworking and went on duty the next morning to find Staff Nurse Bennett in a bad temper and Sister off duty for the day.

Everything went wrong, of course; it always did when Staff Nurse Bennett was there: Trixie dropped things, spilt things and, according to her senior, took twice as long as anyone else to do things. Consequently she was late for her dinner and in a thoroughly bad temper as she nipped smartly along the corridors to the canteen, to encounter Professor van der Brink-Schaaksma, ambling along, an untidy pile of papers under one arm, and, as usual, deep in thought. He glanced at her as she passed him, scurrying along with her head down, to come to a sudden halt when he said, 'Trixie—you are the girl in the brown dress.'

He had turned back to where she was standing. 'I thought that I had seen you somewhere. You fell over...' His sleepy eyes surveyed her. 'You are a friend of Margaret's, to whose party I was invited? It seems unlikely.'

Before she could close her astonished mouth and say a word, he nodded his handsome head, gave her a kindly smile and went on his way.

'Well,' said Trixie. 'Well...' All the clever replies she might have made and hadn't flooded into her head. He had probably uttered his thoughts out loud but that didn't make any difference; it was only too apparent that he had compared her with Margaret and found the comparison untenable.

She flounced off into the canteen in quite a nasty temper, rejected the boiled beef and carrots on the menu, pushed prunes and custard round her plate, drank two cups of very strong tea and marched back to the ward where Staff Nurse Bennett, intent on hauling her over the coals for leaving a bowl on the wrong shelf in the treatment-room, was quite bowled over by the usually well-mannered Trixie's begging her to stop nagging. 'You'll be a most awful wife,' said Trixie. 'In fact I doubt if you'll ever get married, everlastingly picking holes in people.'

She had swept away to get a bed ready to admit a new patient, leaving Staff Nurse Bennett speechless.

It was two days later that she overheard Sister Snell telling Staff Nurse Bennett that Professor van der Brink-Schaaksma had gone to Holland. 'Leiden, I believe—to deliver a series of lectures. A pity he is so wrapped up in his work—such a handsome man, too. I did hear that he had an unhappy love-affair some time ago...'

It was disappointing that they moved away and Trixie missed the rest of it. Not that she was in the least interested in the man, she told herself as she made up empty beds. Indeed, she was sorry for him, going around with his head in endocrinal clouds and never without a pile of papers or some weighty tome under one arm. He needed a wife to give him something else to think about. He had, she reflected, been taken with Margaret, and he couldn't be all that old. Late thirties or forty perhaps, and Margaret had fancied him. He was good-looking, with beautiful manners, and probably comfortably off. She wondered where he lived. She was aware that he was fairly frequently at Timothy's, but it didn't take long to go to and fro between Holland and England; he could be living there just as easily as living in London. She had to stop thinking about him then, because the new patient with diabetes was feeling sick, which could be hazardous, for she hadn't been stabilised yet. Trixie abandoned the beds and nipped smartly down the ward to deal with the situation.

October was creeping to its close, getting colder each day, so that the desire to go out in one's off duty became very faint; the pleasant fug in the nurses' sitting-room, with the television turned on and the gas fire up as high as it would go, became the focal point for anyone lucky enough to be off duty.

Trixie, curled up in one of the rather shabby armchairs sleepily watching TV, after a long day's work, a medical book open on her lap but so far unread, closed her eyes. She and Jill had agreed to ask each other questions about the circulatory system, but Jill was already dozing, her mouth slightly open, her cap, which she hadn't bothered to take off, a crumpled ruin sliding over one ear. It would be supper in an hour and the prospect of a pot of tea, a gossip and early bed was very appealing. 'I'm in a comfortable rut,' muttered Trixie as she dropped off.

To be awakened in seconds by Mary Fitzjohn's voice. 'There you are—someone wants you on the phone.' She sniffed in a derogatory way. 'Honestly, what a way to spend an evening—the pair of you. No wonder Jill's getting fat, lolling around.' She turned an accusing eye on to Trixie. 'Hadn't you better answer the phone?'

She went away and Trixie got out of her chair, gave Jill an apologetic smile, and went into the hall and picked up the receiver.

She almost fumbled and dropped it again at the sound of Professor van der Brink-Schaatsma's unhurried voice. 'Trixie? I should like to take you out to dinner. I'll be outside the entrance in half an hour.'

She got her breath back. 'I think you must be mistaken.' She spoke in her sensible way, picturing him engrossed in some learned work or other and half remembering that he was supposed to be taking someone out that evening, forgetful of who it was. 'I'm Trixie.'

'Of course you are.' He sounded testy. 'Is half an hour not long enough?'

'More than enough, only I'm surprised—you don't know me...'

'That is why I am asking you to have dinner with me.'

It was a reasonable answer; besides, supper in the canteen—ham, salad and boiled potatoes since it was Thursday—was hardly a mouth-watering prospect. 'I'll be at the entrance in half an hour,' said Trixie, and the moment she had said it wished that she hadn't.

While she showered, got into the blue crêpe, did her face and hair, which she wound into a chignon, she cogitated over the professor's strange invitation. She was almost ready when she hit on what had to be the reason. He wanted to know more about Margaret. Why hadn't she thought of that before? He had obviously been smitten at the party, probably had been seeing her since then and wanted to talk about her, and who better than a member of the family? She got into her coat—navy-blue wool, by no means new but elegant in a timeless way—thrust her tired feet into her best shoes, crammed things into her clutchbag and went along to the entrance.

Halfway across the entrance hall she paused, suddenly wishing to turn and run, but it was too late; the professor was standing by the door, leaning against the wall, writing something in a notebook, but he glanced up, put the notebook away and came to meet her.

His smile was delightful and she smiled back. 'You were not christened Trixie?' he asked.

It seemed a strange kind of greeting. 'No, Beatrice. My aunt preferred Trixie.'

He nodded. 'Yes, that I believe.' He held the door open for her and led her across the courtyard to where a dark-blue Bentley stood, settled her into it and got in beside her.

There wasn't a great deal of traffic in that part of London at that time of the evening; the rush-hour had passed and there were few taxis or cars for the people who lived around Timothy's ate their suppers and then settled down in front of the telly, and if they were going to the local pub or cinema they walked.

The Bentley slid smoothly away, going westward, and presently joining the more elegant evening traffic, and then, after ten minutes or so, coming to a halt outside the Connaught Hotel.

The professor appeared to be known; Trixie, conscious that the blue crêpe wasn't doing justice to the occasion, followed a waiter to a candlelit table, accepted the sherry she was offered and waited for the professor to say something, to explain...

She was disappointed; he began a rambling conversation about nothing much, pausing only long enough to recommend the lobster mousse, the noisette of lamb with its accompanying tarragon sauce, and, since she was hungry and this was an unexpected treat, she forbore from asking any questions. Only when she had polished off the profiteroles and had handed him his coffee-cup did she ask, 'Why have you asked me to dine with you, Professor? There has to be a reason.' When he didn't answer at once, she prompted, 'I dare say you want to talk about Margaret.'

'Margaret? Oh, your cousin. Why should I wish to know about her?'

Trixie was a girl of sound common sense, but her tongue had been loosened by two glasses of wine on top of the sherry. 'Well, I thought...that is, I thought that you were—well, interested in her—that you might want to talk about her.'

'A charming girl, I have no doubt of that. I wish to talk about you, and may I say that I do not think that Trixie suits you at all; I shall call you Beatrice.'

'Oh, well—if you like. Mother and Father always called me Beatrice; Aunt Alice has always called me Trixie.'

He didn't appear to be listening. Any minute now, thought Trixie, he's going to start making notes—he's probably forgotten where he is.

She nodded her head in confirmation of this thought when he said, 'I am writing a book. It absorbs a good deal of my time, indeed I wish that I could devote my days to it, but it seems it is not possible to do so; there are patients to attend, lectures and consultations—there are things which cannot be put on one side. My social life is another matter. I wish to withdraw from it until such time as I have finished the book, but I find it difficult to refuse invitations to dinner, the theatre and so on. It had crossed my mind that if I had a wife she might deal with that side of my life; act, as it were, as a buffer between me and these distractions. I am aware that from time to time it is obligatory for me to attend some function or other and that I must from time to time entertain my friends. A wife could deal with such matters, however, leaving me free to work on my book.'

Trixie poured more coffee for them both. 'Is it very important to you, this book?'

'To me, yes. And I hope to the medical profession.'

'How much have you written?'

'The first few chapters. There is a good deal of research.'

'Why are you telling me this, Professor?'

Just for a moment he lifted heavy lids and she saw how blue his eyes were. 'I haven't made myself clear? I believe that you would be a most suitable wife, Beatrice.'

She put down her coffee-cup with a hand which shook only slightly.

'Why?'

'I still have not made myself clear? You are quiet, you have a pleasant voice, the patients like you, you are, I gather, popular in the hospital. You do not giggle or shriek with laughter, you dress sensibly, and above all you have no family, for I surmised from my brief visit to your aunt's house that you are very much the poor relation.'

She said drily, 'You have described me very accurately, Professor, only you haven't mentioned my lack of good looks—I am not tall and willowy, indeed I am plump and not in the least pretty.'

He looked surprised. 'I had hardly noticed and I do not think that looks matter.'

'No?' She sounded tart. 'Tell me, Professor, have you no cousin or sister who might act as a buffer between you and your social commitments?'

'Sister? Oh, I have four, all married and living in Holland and as for cousins—yes, I have any number; I cannot remember the names of half of them. No, no, I feel that a wife would solve my problem.' He leaned back in his chair, completely at ease. 'A platonic relationship, naturally—all I would ask of you would be to order my household in such a way that I have a maximum of quiet.'

'Will you still work at Timothy's?'

'Of course. Very shortly I shall be returning to Holland, where I have beds in several hospitals, but coming here at regular intervals and for consultations when necessary.'

'I can't speak any Dutch,' observed Trixie, who had a practical mind.

'You will learn! In any case English is widely spoken.'

She said rather wildly, 'We're talking as though I've agreed to—your proposal, but I haven't.'

'I would hardly expect you to do so at a moment's notice; you are far too sensible a young woman to do that. I leave it to you to consider the matter at your leisure.'

He was staring at her, looking, for the moment, not in the least absent-minded. 'Yes, well...but I don't think...that is, it's all rather unusual.' She closed her eyes for a second and opened them again. He was still there; she wasn't dreaming. 'If you don't mind, I think I'd like to go back to Timothy's.'

He drove her back, talking in a desultory manner about this and that, and never said another word about his astonishing proposal. She allowed herself to be helped out of the car, feeling bewildered, and stammered her awkward thanks before hurrying away to the nurses' home. He hadn't said a word about seeing her again, she thought as she tore off her clothes and jumped into bed. Probably, when they did meet again, he would have forgotten the whole episode. She began to go over the evening and fell asleep halfway through, telling herself that something would happen anyway.

CHAPTER TWO

NOTHING happened, at least nothing to do with Trixie and the professor. A week went by and a most unsatisfactory week it was: Staff Nurse Bennett's dislike of her manifested itself in a dozen annoying ways; off duty changed at the last minute when Sister Snell had days off, going late to meals because of some errand which really had to be run, constant criticism of whatever she was doing on the ward. Trixie's temper, usually good, had become badly frayed. It was fortunate that she had days off even though she was late going off duty that evening. She left the ward and started down the stone staircase to the floor below. She would have supper and go to bed early and decide what she was going to do with her precious two days. The parks, she thought; a good walk would improve her temper. November, it seemed, was to be a sunny crisp month, and she needed the exercise. She loitered along, happily engaged in her plans, when the professor's voice from behind and above her startled her into missing her footing. He plucked her upright and fell into step beside her.

'I could have broken a leg,' said Trixie with asperity. 'Creeping up behind me like that.' She eventually remembered to whom she was speaking and then mumbled, 'Sorry, sir, but you startled me.'

He didn't appear to hear her. 'You have days off, Beatrice?'

They had reached the floor below and she turned to look up at him. 'Yes.'

He eyed her narrowly. 'You are pale and I think rather cross. Has it been a bad week?'

'Awful. I shall never be a good nurse, Staff Nurse Bennett says so.'

He smiled faintly. 'She is quite right,' and at her indignant gasp, 'I shall explain...'

He was interrupted by one of the path lab assistants. 'Sir, they are waiting for you. Dr Gillespie is quite ready...'

The professor waved a large hand. 'Yes, yes, I am on my way. I will be with you in a moment.' When the man went back up the stairs, he went on walking beside Trixie, who was bent on getting away from him at the earliest possible moment. Halfway across the vast landing she stopped.

'You're going the wrong way, Professor,' she reminded him gently.

'Yes, yes, I dare say I am, but I wish to talk to you.'

'They're waiting for you,' she pointed out patiently. 'I should think it's urgent.'

He said at once, 'Ah, yes! A most interesting case; a tumour of the medulla—I believe it to be a phaeochromocytoma. This will cause hypertension...'

Trixie, her eyes popping out of her head and quite out of her depth, put a hand on one large coat sleeve. If she didn't stop him now he'd ramble on happily about the adrenal glands. 'Sir—sir, you have to go back upstairs. Oh, do go to the path lab. Dr Gillespie is waiting for you.'

He wasn't listening. 'You see, the hypertension will give rise to irregular cardiac rhythm...' He glanced down at her. 'Why are you looking like that, Beatrice?'

She neither knew nor cared what she looked like. 'The path lab,' she urged him.

'Ah, yes. I have an appointment there.' He patted her arm in a kindly fashion and turned to go back up the staircase. 'Be outside at nine o'clock tomorrow morning; we will have a day in the country.'

Trixie asked faintly, 'Will we?' but he had already gone, two steps at a time. She glimpsed his great back disappearing on the landing above.

She started on her way again to be brought to a halt by his voice, loud and clear enough for the whole hospital to hear. He was hanging over the balustrade with the path lab assistant hovering anxiously.

'Wear something warm, Beatrice. I have a wish to breathe the sea air.'

He disappeared, leaving her to continue across the landing and down another flight of stairs and so to her room. She sat down on the bed to think. A day by the sea would be wonderful and the professor was a charming companion, if somewhat unmindful of his surroundings from time to time. From these reflections her thoughts progressed naturally enough to the important question as to what to wear. Not a winter coat, it wasn't cold enough, and her old quilted jacket wouldn't do in case they had a meal somewhere. It would have to be the elderly Jaeger suit, timeless in cut, its tweed of the best quality, but, to a discerning female eye, out of date. The professor probably hadn't a discerning eye, indeed he had observed that she dressed sensibly, which, considering that he had only seen her in uniform and the brown velvet and blue crêpe, proved her point. It would have to be the tweed. This important decision having been made, she felt free to wonder why he wanted to spend a day with her. She refused to take seriously his remarks about her being a suitable wife. He must have friends here in London even if he was Dutch; he had seemed on very easy terms with Colonel Vosper and surely if he wanted a day out he would have chosen someone like Margaret, guaranteed to be an amusing companion besides having a pretty face and the right clothes.

She got out of her uniform slowly, and, no longer wishing for her supper, got into a dressing-gown and went along to the kitchenette to make a pot of tea and eat the rest of the rich tea biscuits left in the packet. Waiting for the kettle to boil, she put her name down for bread and butter and marmalade for her breakfast, which the nurses' home maid would bring over and leave in the kitchenette. She was hunting round for milk when several of her friends came off duty after supper.

'You're not ill, are you?' asked Lucy. 'You never miss meals.'

'I'm fine, I wasn't hungry. I've got days off anyway.'

She wished she hadn't said that, for Mary asked in her nosy way, 'Going home, are you?'

'No.'

'Got a date?'

She didn't need to think of an answer for someone said, gently teasing, 'Of course she has. The Governor of the Bank of England; lunch off a gold plate at the Ritz and dinner and dancing with minor royalty...'

There was a chorus of laughter and Mary said huffily, 'You all talk such nonsense.' She thumped down her mug and went away, and presently the rest of them wandered away to wash their hair, do their nails and argue as to who should have the hairdrier first. Trixie nipped into one of the bathrooms before anyone else had laid claim to it, and soaked in the bath, wishing that she had said a firm 'no' to the professor's invitation—not an invitation, really, more an order which he had taken for granted would be obeyed. She was pondering ways and means of letting him know that she wouldn't be able to join him in the morning when repeated impatient thumps on the door forced her to get out of the bath.

'You've been in there hours,' said Mary. 'You're the colour of a lobster too. You'll probably get a chill; a good thing you've got days off.'

Trixie took the pins out of her hair and let it fall in a soft brown curtain around her shoulders. 'Yes, isn't it?' she agreed cheerfully, and went off to drink more tea with such of her friends as hadn't gone to bed. Later, in her room, curled up in her bed, she found the chapter on endocrinology and read it carefully. The professor would probably discuss the subject nearest his heart and it might help to sustain a sensible conversation if she had some idea of the subject. She had had several lectures on it; indeed, the professor himself had delivered one of them, using so many long words that she had dozed off halfway through and had had to be prodded awake when he had finished.

It took her a little time to go to sleep, her head being full of any number of facts concerning ductless glands all nicely muddled.

In the light of an early November morning, the whole thing seemed absurd. Nevertheless, Trixie ate her toast and drank her tea and got into the tweed, did her hair and face with extra care, and, as nine o'clock struck, went down to the front entrance.

The professor was there, sharing a copy of the *Sun* with the head porter. He handed his portion back and went to meet her. His good morning was cheerful if brief. 'The variety of newspapers in this country is wide,' he told her. 'I do not as a rule read anything other than *The Times* or the *Telegraph* but I must admit that the paper I have just been reading is, to say the least, stimulating, though I must admit that the advertisements in the Dutch daily papers are even more revealing.'

He ushered her into the car and got in beside her but made no attempt to drive away. 'It is an interesting fact,' he informed her, 'that I find myself able to talk to you without inhibitions.' He didn't wait for her reply. 'Do you know the east coast at all? There is a most interesting village there, once a town swallowed by the sea; it is National Trust property so that we can, if we wish, walk for miles.'

Trixie said faintly, 'It sounds very pleasant. I don't know that part of the country at all.'

He started the car and after that had very little to say, not that there was much to say about the Mile End Road, Leytonstone, Wanstead Flats and so on to the A12, but when they reached Chelmsford he turned north and took the road through Castle Hedingham and on to Lavenham, and there he stopped at the Swan Hotel, remarking that it was time they had a cup of coffee. The road was a quiet one, the country was wide and the town was old and charming. Trixie had given up serious thoughts; she was enjoying herself, and, although they had had but desultory talk, she felt very much at ease with her companion. She got out of the car and sat in the old inn, drinking her coffee and listening to his informed talk about the town.

'Do you know this part of England well?' she asked.

'I do, yes. You see, it reminds me of my own country.' He smiled at her and passed his cup for more coffee.

'Wouldn't you like to live in Holland?'

'I do for a great deal of the time. I have, as it were, a foot in both camps. Do you know the Continent at all?'

'My aunt and uncle took me to France while I was still at school. Paris.'

She remembered that she hadn't enjoyed it much because she had had to do what Margaret wanted all the time and Margaret had no wish to look at old buildings and churches, only wanted to walk down the Rue de Rivoli and spend hours in the shops. 'That's all,' she added flatly. 'I expect you've travelled a lot?'

'Well, yes. I go where I'm needed.'

They drove on presently and now he took the car through a network of side roads, missing Stowmarket and not joining the main road again until they had almost reached the coast, and presently they turned into a narrow country road which led eventually to a tree-shaded area where the professor parked the car. 'This is where we get out and walk,' he told Trixie, and got out to open her door. She could see the sea now and the village behind a shingle bank and low cliffs. It looked lonely and bleak under the grey sky, but the path they took was sheltered and winding, leading them into the village street. 'Lunch?' asked the professor, and took her by the arm and urged her into the Ship Inn.

He had been there before; he was greeted cheerfully by the stout cheerful man behind the bar, asked if he would like his usual and what would the young lady have?

Trixie settled for coffee and a ploughman's lunch and sat down near the open fireplace. While she ate it, the professor talked of the history of the village, once a Saxon and then a Roman town, long swallowed up by the sea. Between mouthfuls of cheese he assured her that the bells of numerous churches long since drowned by the encroaching seas were still to be heard tolling beneath the waves. 'There is a monastery along the cliffs; we will walk there presently and on to the Heath.'

They set out in a while with a strong wind blowing into their faces and the North Sea grey below the cliffs. The surge of the waves breaking on the shingle was almost as loud as the wind soughing among the trees. The professor had tucked her hand into his and was marching along at a good pace. It was evident that he envisaged a long walk. She thanked heaven for sensible shoes and saved her breath. They didn't talk much until they were in sight of the coastguard cottages and beyond the bird reserve and the wide sweep of the coastline; indeed, it was so windy that just breathing normally was a bit of an effort. Trixie came to a thankful halt at last and the professor turned her round and studied her face.

'That is better. I think that nursing is not a suitable life for you.'

'Oh, do you? That's what Staff Nurse Bennett says; that I'll never make a good nurse.'

'An unkind young woman.' He stared down at her face, nicely rosy from the wind and the sea air. 'It has occurred to me that I have been over-hasty in broaching the subject of our marriage. Nevertheless, I hope that you have given it your consideration. Perhaps you have a boyfriend of your own or you may not wish to marry?'

His voice was quiet and very faintly accented.

'Me? A boyfriend? Heavens, no. At least,' she hesitated, 'before I started my training, there was a man who was one of Margaret's friends—Aunt Alice would have liked him for a son-in-law, but for some reason he—he liked me instead of Margaret. That's why I started nursing...'

It was a meagre enough explanation but the professor seemed to understand it. 'I see—you say "out of sight, out of mind", do you not?'

'Yes, but I didn't like him anyway...'

'You have no objection to being married, do you?'

'None at all,' she told him soberly, and thought what a strange conversation they were having. Not even a glimmer of romance either, but the professor didn't strike her as a romantic man; his work was his life, and she suspected that his social life was something he regarded as an unwelcome necessity.

'So you will consider becoming my wife? I have already explained to you that all I ask is peace and quiet so that I may write whenever I have the time. You will not mind being left to your own devices? There will be times when I shall be obliged to attend dinner parties and similar occasions, but I shall rely upon you to deal with any entertaining which I may be obliged to do from time to time; to deal with the tiresome details, answer the telephone calls and return the visits which are so distracting.'

He looked away from her to the grey sea, and Trixie said in her matter-of-fact way, 'I expect you are very sought after—there must be lots of girls who would like to marry you.'

He didn't look at her, although he smiled a little. 'You would not mind acting as my guardian? I find that young women can be very ruthless in getting what they want.'

It would be worth trying, thought Trixie—a handsome man, still quite young, well known in his profession, well off, she supposed, able to give his wife the comforts of life. All he wanted was to work and write his book. He said to surprise her, 'I should like to fall in love—it is a long time ago since I did that and now my life is so full and perhaps I am too old.'

'Pooh,' said Trixie. 'Age hasn't anything to do with it. Get that book written and then you'll have time to look around you.'

He did glance at her then, although she couldn't read the look in his eyes beneath their dropping lids. 'But I shall be married to you.'

'Ah, yes—but not—not . . . that is, divorce is very easy these days.'

He took her hands in his. 'You do understand, don't you? My work is so very important to me and it has been so for years. So will you marry me, Beatrice?'

'Yes. I think it might be a good idea. I'm not likely to get asked by anyone else. I like you and I feel easy with you, although I don't know you at all, do I? I will really try to be the sort of wife you want.'

'I'm a selfish man . . .'

'No. You are driven by your urge to do something you feel you must—like Scott going to the Pole or Hilary climbing Everest.' She smiled at him. 'I'll guard you like a dragon.'

'I believe you will.' He flung a great arm around her shoulders and felt her shiver in the wind. 'You're cold— how thoughtless of me. We'll go back. We can stop for tea at Lawshall; there's a pleasant hotel there.' He glanced at his watch. 'I need to be back at Timothy's by seven o'clock—I'm admitting a woman with exophthalmos, a most interesting case, and I want to make sure that the special treatment is started immediately. I dare say you haven't come across a case—it is a question of controlling the hyperthyroidism . . .'

They had begun to walk back and they were going up the path to where the car had been parked before the finer points of the condition had been explained. The professor stopped so suddenly that Trixie almost over-balanced. 'Oh, my dear Beatrice, I had quite lost myself, do forgive me, I tend to forget...'

It was at that moment, looking up into his concerned face, that Trixie fell in love with him.

The knowledge rendered her speechless but only for a moment, for at the same moment she had realised that this was something which was going to happen time and again and she would have to get used to it. She said calmly, 'I found it most interesting and you don't need to apologise, now or ever. The poor woman—I do so hope you'll be able to cure her.'

They had reached the car and were leaning against its elegant bonnet.

'I shall do what I can; if the Diotroxin and the radio-therapy fail to halt it, then it will have to be tarsorrhaphy. I will explain about that...'

He was lost again, deep in the subject nearest his heart, and Trixie, getting colder by the minute in the now chilly wind, listened willingly because she liked the sound of his deep voice and he was treating her as someone in whom he could confide. When, at length, he paused, she said warmly, 'Oh, I do expect you must be anxious to get back to Timothy's and get started on her.'

He opened the car door and ushered her in, and she at once sank thankfully into the comfort of the soft leather. As he got in beside her she said, 'We won't stop for tea if you want to get back.'

He patted her knee in an impersonal manner and sent electric shocks all over her. 'No, no, there's time enough. We shall be back well before seven o'clock; that should give you time to tidy yourself while I'm on the ward.

I'll get someone to ring the nurses' home when I'm ready and we can meet in the hall.'

She turned her head to look at his calm profile. 'Meet you? In the hall? Why?'

'I told Mies to have dinner ready for half-past eight...'

'Who's Mies?'

'My housekeeper. I've a small house near Harley Street; when I'm over here I have the use of some consulting-rooms there.' He slowed the car. 'Here we are at Lawshall.'

The hotel was small, comfortable and welcoming. They ate crumpets swimming in butter and rich fruit cake and drank the contents of the teapot between them, and the professor didn't mention the endocrine glands once. He talked pleasantly about a great many things, but he didn't mention their own situation either and Trixie, bursting with unspoken little questions, made all the right kind of remarks and thought about how much she loved him.

They drove on again presently, to reach the hospital with ten minutes to spare. The professor saw her out of the car and walked with her to the entrance. 'I'll wait here,' he told her. 'I expect to be about an hour.'

He gave her a friendly pat on the shoulder and she said, 'Very well,' and walked away towards the nurses' home entrance because she suspected that he was hiding impatience. In her room she got out of the tweed and combed through her wardrobe, intent on finding something suitable to wear. Not the velvet or the crêpe; she kept those for rare parties. There was a perfectly plain jersey dress buried behind her summer dresses. She had had it for years because it was such a useful colour, nutmeg brown. It had a high round neck and long sleeves and a wide, rather long skirt.

She was ready long before the hour was up so she went down to the sitting-room, relieved to find no one there, and read a yesterday's newspaper someone had left there. She was doggedly working her way through a long political speech when the warden poked her head round the door.

'Nurse Doveton, Professor van der Brink-Schaaksma will be ready in five minutes.' She added severely, 'I must say I am surprised.' She eyed Trixie's heightened colour and sniffed. 'I didn't know that you knew him.'

Trixie was pulling on her gloves and making last-minute inspections of her face and handbag. The warden was a sour lady of uncertain years, overflowing with unspoken criticisms of the younger nurses and disliked by them all. Happy in her own small heaven, Trixie wanted everyone else to be happy too.

'I expect you are,' she said blithely. 'I'm a bit surprised myself.'

He was there waiting, and he came across the hall to meet her.

'Is everything all right?' she wanted to know. 'Has she settled in?'

'Yes, and I think that she will be a good patient.' He opened the door and they went out to the car and got in.

'Have you finished for the day?'

He drove out of the forecourt and edged into the evening traffic. 'Yes. There is nothing much I can do till the morning. I shall have to see her doctor—she's a private patient—and talk things over with my registrar.'

She had the feeling that just for the moment he had forgotten that she was there. She sat quietly as he drove across London until they reached the quieter streets, lined with tall old houses, leading to equally quiet squares, each with its enclosed garden in the centre.

'You're very quiet,' said the professor suddenly.

'I was thinking how different this is from Timothy's...'

'Indeed yes. My house in Holland is different again. In a small village near Leiden—very quiet. You like the country?'

'Yes, very much.'

He had turned into a narrow street lined with Georgian houses and he stopped halfway down. He turned to look at her. 'This is where I live, Beatrice.' Then he got out and opened her door. She stood and looked around her for a moment; the houses were what she supposed an estate agent would describe as bijou and those she could see clearly in the lamplit street were immaculate as to paint and burnished brass-work on their front doors, and the house they approached was immaculate too with a fanlight over the black-painted door which was reached by three shallow steps guarded by a thin rail. There was a glow of light behind the bow window and bright light streaming from its basement.

The professor opened the door and stood aside for her to go in, still silent, and she went past him into the long narrow hall, its walls white and hung with paintings, red carpet underfoot and a small side-table against one wall. Halfway down its length a curved staircase led to the floor above and there were several doors on the opposite side. It was the door at the end of the hall which was opened, allowing a short stout elderly woman to enter.

The professor was taking Trixie's coat. 'Mies...' He spoke to her in Dutch and then said, 'Mies speaks English but she's a little shy about it. She understands very well, though.'

Trixie held out a hand and said how do you do, and smiled at the wrinkled round face. Mies could have been any age; her hair was dark and glossy and her small bright eyes beamed above plump cheeks, but the hand she offered was misshapen with arthritis and her voice was that of an old woan. Her smile was warm and so was her greeting. 'It is a pleasure, miss.' She took Trixie's coat from the professor, spoke to him in her own language and trotted off.

'In here,' said the professor, and swept Trixie through the nearest door and into a room at the front of the house. Not a large room, but furnished in great good taste with comfortable chairs and a wide sofa, small lamp tables and a display cabinet filled with silver and porcelain against one wall. There was a brisk fire burning in the polished steel fireplace and sitting before it was a large tabby cat accompanied by a dog of no particular parentage. The cat took no notice of them but the dog jumped up, delighted to see them.

Trixie bent to pat the woolly head. 'He's yours?'

'Mies and I share him. I can't take him to and fro from Holland—sometimes I am away from here for weeks on end, months even—so he lives here with her and I enjoy his company when I'm here. He's called Caesar.'

'Why?' She sat down in the chair he had offered.

'He came—from nowhere presumably, he saw us and decided to stay and conquered Mies's kind heart within the first hour or so.'

He sat down opposite her and the cat got up and went to sit on the arm of his chair.

'And the cat?'

'Gumbie.'

Trixie laughed, 'Oh, I know—from TS Eliot's *Old Possum's Book of Practical Cats*.' She added in a surprised voice, 'Have you read it?'

'Oh, yes. I have a copy in my study. Gumbie belongs to Mies; the pair of them make splendid company when I am away.'

'Mies doesn't mind being alone here?'

'There is a housemaid, Gladys. They get on very well together.' He got up. 'May I get you a drink? I think there's time before dinner.'

They sat in a companionable silence for a few minutes then Trixie asked, 'Do you have to go back to the hospital this evening?'

'I shall drive you back later and make sure that all is well with my patient. I have an out-patients clinic in the morning, which probably means more admissions, and a ward-round in the afternoon.'

'You don't plan to go back to Holland just yet?'

'Not for some time, but I hope to before Christmas. I've some examining to do in December and a seminar in January so I shall be over there for some time. I come over fairly frequently. It is a very short journey by plane and I need only stay for a few hours.'

Mies came to tell them that dinner was on the table then and during the meal the conversation, to Trixie's disappointment, never once touched on themselves. Had the professor a father and mother living? she wondered, spooning artichoke soup and making polite remarks about the east coast and their day out and going on with the braised duck with wine sauce to a few innocuous remarks about the weather and the delights of autumn, and then with the lemon soufflé, fortified by two glasses of the white Burgundy she had drunk on top of the sherry, and with her tongue nicely loosened, she allowed it to run away with her.

'I don't know your name or how old you are or where you live exactly. I should have thought that by now you would have been married. You must have been in love…'

She tossed off the last of the wine and added, 'Of course you don't have to tell me if you don't want to, only I'd rather like to know, because...' She stopped just in time, going pale at the thought that she had been on the point of telling him that she had fallen in love with him. She finished lamely, 'Well, of course you don't have to tell me. I didn't mean to be rude.'

'Not rude—you have every right to know, in the circumstances. Additionally, one day when we have the leisure you must tell me all about yourself. Now let us go back to the drawing-room and have our coffee and I will answer your questions.'

Once more by the fire with the coffee-tray between them, with Caesar's head resting on the professor's beautifully polished shoes and Gumbie curled up on Trixie's lap, he observed, 'Now, let me see—what was your first question? My name—Krijn, I'll spell it.' He did so. 'It is a Friese name because my family come from Friesland. I'm thirty-eight—does that seem old to you? I have a mother and father, they live in Friesland and my four sisters are younger than I and married, and yes, I have been in love—a very long time ago; I think that you do not have to worry about that. She is happily married in South America, leading the kind of life I would have been unable to give her. I must confess that since then I have never thought seriously about marriage and I am perfectly content with my way of life—or have been until recently when I realised that a bachelor is very vulnerable, and, having given the matter due thought, marriage seemed the right answer.' He smiled at her. 'Do I seem too frank? I do not intend to hurt your feelings, Beatrice, but you are such a sensible girl there is no need to wrap up plain facts in fancy speeches.'

She longed to tell him how wrong he was; the most sensible girl in the world would never object to fancy speeches, but all she said was, 'Thank you for telling me. I'm sorry you—your love-life was blighted...' It sounded old-fashioned in her ears and she felt a fool, but his face remained placid although his eyes, half-hidden beneath their lids, held amusement. The amusement was kindly; he liked her, he felt at ease with her and she would act as a buffer between him and the determined efforts of his friends and acquaintances to get him married to any one of the attractive girls he met at their houses. He would have more time for his book...and in return she would have anything she wanted within reason and lead the kind of life she deserved. He remembered the strange pang he had felt when she had fallen down in the ward...

'As soon as I am free I will call upon your uncle and aunt. There is no reason why we shouldn't be married within the next few weeks, is there?'

The mere thought of it sent her heart rocking. 'No, no, none at all.'

'Good. I'll let you know when I'm free for a day or two. You should have the privilege of choosing the day, should you not? So I will tell you when I can arrange to be away and give you a choice. Will that do?'

She nodded. 'I have to give a month's notice.'

'Don't worry about that. I'll arrange for you to leave whenever you wish. You will wish to go to your aunt's house?'

'Well, I'm not sure if it would be convenient. Up to now I've only gone when I'm invited...'

'In that case we will have a quiet wedding and you can stay with some friends of mine for a few days before we marry. In a church?'

'Please. But will they want me?'

'They'll be delighted. Your aunt and uncle and Margaret will wish to be at the wedding?'

She took a deep breath. 'Would you mind awfully if we just got married—just us and two witnesses, I mean, then I could go straight to the church from the hospital? That's unless you wanted your family to come to the wedding?'

'I hadn't intended asking them. We could go over for a couple of days so that you might meet them and I should very much prefer a quiet ceremony if that is what you want.'

'Yes, it is. I mean it's not quite like an ordinary marriage, is it?' Regret that the wedding of every girl's dreams wasn't to be for her sent sudden tears to her eyes, but she had no intention of crying. She was going to marry the man she loved and that was all that mattered. He was pleased, she could see that. She glanced at the clock and suggested in her quiet voice that she should go back to Timothy's, and tried not to mind when he made no effort to keep her. She suspected that, the question of his wedding having been settled, he could turn with relief to his patient's problems.

He bade her a friendly goodnight in the hospital, waiting until she had gone through the nurses' home door before going to the wards, forgetting her the moment he reached them. As for Trixie, she undressed slowly, suddenly tired—which was a good thing, for her thoughts weren't entirely happy—so that she slept before she began to worry.

CHAPTER THREE

SOMEHOW with the morning Trixie's worries had disappeared. She got up and wandered along to the kitchen to make tea, since she had a second day off, and although she hadn't handed in her name for breakfast the home maid fetched her bread and butter and marmalade. She took the lot back on a tray and got into bed and several of her friends poked their heads round the door on their way to their own breakfast to wish themselves in her place and ask what she was going to do with her day.

Yesterday still loomed large in her thoughts; she hadn't given a thought to today. 'Nothing—just potter. Do some window-shopping and be back here for tea, most likely.'

'How about the flicks this evening?' asked Lucy. 'See you then.'

There wasn't any point in lying in bed once she had gobbled up her bread and butter. She got up again and dressed and presently left Timothy's and got a bus bound for Regent Street. The rush-hour was over but there were plenty of shoppers strolling from one window to the next. Trixie joined them, her small nose close to the glass, lost in a pleasant dream wherein she was able to buy anything she wanted without having to bear in mind the fact that it would have to last for a year or two. If she married the professor—she repeated the 'if' to herself—presumably she would be able to indulge her taste to a certain extent. She supposed that he was fairly well-off and she would have an allowance for clothes. Aunt Alice did; so did Margaret.

She wandered along and turned into Bond Street, peering at the exquisite clothes in the boutiques and wondering if he would see her that evening. He had told her that he would be busy all day, but surely he would be free later in the day? Perhaps he would take her to his home again and they would have dinner together—the duck had been delicious... She suddenly felt hungry and the sight of a small café down a side street sent her hurrying to it. She hadn't much money—pay-day was still a week away—but she ordered coffee and a bun and then, refreshed, continued her window-shopping until it was time to go to Oxford Street and buy herself lunch in the cafeteria in BHS. There was still the afternoon to fill in. She took a bus to the National Gallery and wandered around the galleries studying the paintings. There weren't many people there and she went from one vast room to the next, a small lonely figure but quite content. She had always hoped that she would meet a man she would love and want to marry, but she hadn't had much hope of doing so and certainly had had little hope of any man wanting to marry her; now her dearest dream had come true. Suddenly anxious to get back to Timothy's in case he was looking for her, she joined a bus queue and went back to Regent Street and then caught another bus to Timothy's.

It was dusk already and there was a damp mist. The many lights shining from Timothy's' windows merely served to show up the shabbiness of the surrounding streets. Trixie hardly noticed that; she bounced through the entrance doors and started across the hall towards the nurses' home entrance. She was passing the porter's lodge when Murgatroyd, the head porter, put his head through the little window.

'Nurse Doveton? There's a letter for you.'

She recognised the almost illegible writing on the envelope. It was the same scrawl as his signature on the forms she had so often been bidden to take to various departments. She beamed at Murgatroyd, wished him a good evening, and sped to her room, already wondering what to wear.

The note, when she opened the envelope, was brief and a poor example of the kind of letter a man would write to his future bride. It stated in a businesslike manner that the professor would be in Holland for the next few days and signed it with his initials.

Trixie read it for a second time, telling herself that possibly he had been in a great hurry when he had written it. At least he was honest, she reminded herself; he liked her—enough to marry her—but he wasn't going to pretend to stronger feelings. Something she would have to get used to. 'After all,' she said to herself, 'if I hadn't fallen in love with him I don't suppose I would have minded in the least.'

She put the letter under her pillow and went downstairs to the sitting-room and had tea with the other nurses who were off duty, and presently a bunch of them went along to the local cinema, and when the film was over they bought fish and chips and had their supper, crowded into Trixie's room, discussing the film and the latest fashions over endless cups of tea.

When they had all gone, she had a bath and got into bed and read the letter once more before putting it back under the pillow. Perhaps she was making a mistake. She could tell him so and leave Timothy's and not see him again and although he might be vexed at having his plans spoilt he wouldn't break his heart, whereas hers would break. Her eyes filled with tears at the very idea of never seeing him any more. She slipped a hand under the pillow, held the letter tightly and fell asleep.

Staff Nurse Bennett was in an evil mood the next morning. Trixie could do nothing right; she was slow, clumsy, careless and entirely lacking in common sense. It was therefore something of a relief when a ward orderly interrupted a particularly harsh diatribe concerning her faults to say that Nurse Doveton was to go to Sister's office.

'Now what have you done?' asked Staff Nurse Bennett fiercely.

Trixie didn't bother to answer. It would at least make a change to be chastened by another voice. She tapped on the door and was bidden to enter.

'There is a telephone call for you, Nurse. I do not, as a rule, allow nurses to take private calls on the ward, but it seems that I have to make an exception in your case. Pray be as brief as you can.'

Sister sailed away, looking annoyed and curious at the same time.

Aunt Alice, thought Trixie, putting a reluctant hand on the receiver. Quite a while ago, when Trixie had first started her training, Aunt Alice had telephoned her on the ward, and the ward sister had reduced her to silent misery at the very idea of junior nurses receiving calls on the ward. Trixie had extracted a promise from Aunt Alice that after all that she would never telephone unless it was a matter of dire emergency. She put the receiver to her ear, expecting to hear her aunt's voice warning her that Uncle William had had a stroke or that Margaret had been in a car accident with one of her young men.

'You had my note?' asked the professor without so much as a hello.

She was too surprised to utter and he added a shade testily, 'Well?'

'Yes—yes, thank you.' She drew a breath. 'I didn't expect——'

He cut in ruthlessly. 'I shall be back in two days' time. It might be a good idea to visit your aunt and uncle then. When are you off duty?'

'After five o'clock.'

'Good, will you let them know that you wish to see them? At what time do they dine?'

'Eight o'clock, but they might be going out.'

'In which case perhaps you can arrange to see them at seven o'clock?'

'All right. Do you want me to tell them about us, that is, that you'll be with me?'

'I think not. I'll be in touch when I return.' He rang off with a quick goodbye, and she told herself that very likely he was terribly busy. She went back to the ward. There was no sign of Sister, and Staff Nurse Bennett had gone for her coffee-break. Trixie went back to her interrupted task of getting old Mrs Perch, recovering from a stroke, out of her bed and into a chair. The other two nurses were on the other side of the ward making beds.

'Was it a blasting?' asked one of them.

'No. Nothing like that.' She was saved from saying any more by Sister's return.

She telephoned Aunt Alice the next day during her dinner-break, and that lady asked at once why she should want to see her and her uncle. 'I hope you don't want to borrow money, Trixie,' said Aunt Alice, who had plenty of her own but disliked sharing it. 'Or are you in trouble of some kind? I sincerely trust that that is not the case.'

'No, nothing like that,' said Trixie. 'I'll explain tomorrow evening.'

'We are dining out, so try to be punctual. Margaret is going to the ball at the Dorchester; I doubt if she will have the time to talk to you—she will have to dress.'

Trixie rang off for there was really no more to say. It would have to be said tomorrow, but the professor could deal with that. She hoped that he would allow his undoubtedly brilliant mind to forget his work for the moment and concentrate on what might possibly be a ticklish situation. Aunt Alice wasn't going to like the idea of her plain and unassuming ward marrying before her own lovely daughter. A good thing the wedding was going to be so quiet.

The professor came on to the ward the following afternoon, accompanied by Dr Gillespie and his housemen. He greeted Sister Snell with his usual courtesy, nodded to Staff Nurse Bennett and engrossed himself at once in his patient's treatment. Trixie, after the first surprise, took care not to look at him and since kindly providence put it into Sister's head to send her to the records office for some old notes she was able to absent herself from the ward for ten minutes or more, by which time he was finished with his patient and was standing in the middle of the ward conferring with Dr Gillespie while Sister hovered. He took the notes with an absent, 'Thank you, Nurse,' his mind obviously fully occupied with Mrs Downs's glands, and Trixie, with a heightened colour, took herself off to tidy that lady and sit her up in bed again. She managed to make that last long enough for the men to leave the ward and then, urged crossly by Staff Nurse Bennett not to be all day about such a simple task, set about feeding old Mrs Masters who was no longer able to do it for herself.

She was sent to her tea presently and she went the long way round to the canteen to see if there was a note for her at the porter's lodge. There was no note but Murgatroyd looked up as she reached it.

'I was to tell you,' he said stolidly, 'to be here, in this place, at quarter to seven sharp.' He cocked a knowing eye at her. 'OK?'

Trixie heaved a sigh of relief. 'Oh, yes, thank you, Murgatroyd.' She gave him a rather shy smile and he grinned at her. What Professor van der Brink-Schaaksma saw in this mouselike girl he couldn't understand, but there was no accounting for tastes, and the pair of them were nice, civil too, which was more than could be said for some of them.

Trixie walked on air to her tea, gobbled bread and butter and drank tea in a dreamlike state which left her companions puzzled, and went back to the ward for the last half-hour of her day's work. It was a little longer than that, for Staff Nurse Bennett wasn't one to allow a nurse to go off duty punctually—she called it clock-watching. All the same, Trixie was a mere fifteen minutes behind time and quarter to seven was still nicely remote.

She showered, did her face and hair with extreme care and got into the tweed suit. It was a chilly evening and already quite dark, and she thought it unlikely that the professor would suggest taking her anywhere after their visit. He had made it plain that any leisure he had would be devoted to his writing. She quite wondered how long it would take him to write the book, and, a little uneasily, wondered what would happen when it was finished. He wouldn't need anyone to guard him then...

She was punctual but he was already there, talking to Murgatroyd. He came to meet her as she crossed the hall. 'Ah, Beatrice,' he took her hand, 'what a comfortable person you are, doing what I ask without fuss and not asking tedious questions. You have arranged to go to your aunt?'

'Yes. They are going out to dinner and I was asked to be punctual.'

'Well, what we have to tell them will not take long, will it? Will they wish to discuss our wedding, do you suppose?'

She said bleakly, 'No, I don't think so. I think that perhaps Aunt Alice may be a bit annoyed...'

'Because you are marrying before your cousin?'

'Yes, and—and I think you must be very eligible. I mean you could have married anyone, taken your pick!' She looked up at him with a small worried frown.

He said without conceit, 'Yes, I could, but I do not want a wife who is forever wishing to go out to dine or attending endless parties. Once acquaintances have realised that we prefer a quiet life they will invite us less frequently. Of course I have a number of friends both here and in Holland.'

'The medical profession?'

'Yes, very largely.'

Trixie thought privately that she would need to buy the best medical dictionary there was—his friends would doubtless find long discussions about the human frame and its ailments a pleasant way of spending an evening. If she hadn't loved him so much she would have backed out while there was still time.

They got into the car and drove to Highgate and as they stood in the porch waiting for the door to be opened he took her hand in a comforting clasp. 'Just tell them why we're here and leave the rest to me,' he told her.

The maid who answered their knock was new but then Aunt Alice never could keep her domestic staff. Trixie said in her quiet voice, 'Good evening. Mrs Doveton is expecting me—Miss Doveton.'

The maid nodded in a surly fashion and stood aside for them to go into the hall to be greeted by Aunt Alice's voice saying loudly through the half-open drawing-room door, 'Trixie, come in, come in. I do hope whatever it is you have to tell us won't take too long—this really is most inconvenient...'

Aunt Alice was sitting by the fire, half turned away from it and she didn't bother to look round as Trixie and the professor went into the room. 'Your uncle and I are dining at the Grahams' and as I have told you so many times punctuality on social occasions is so important... I suppose——' She turned her head then and saw them standing together, her hand still in his, and she stopped being Aunt Alice and became the polished hostess on the instant. 'Why, Professor van der Brink-Schaaksma, what a delightful surprise. I suppose you have given Trixie a lift? I heard that you sometimes give consultations at the hospital where she works. How very kind of you—you must have a drink...'

His 'Good evening, Mrs Doveton,' was gravely polite and he refused the drink. 'We must on no account make you late for your dinner party,' he added smoothly. 'Beatrice and I have come on the briefest of visits in order to tell you that we are to be married very shortly.'

Aunt Alice went an unbecoming crimson and then very pale. 'Married... Trixie, marry you? How on earth...?' She pulled herself together. 'Well, this is a surprise, but of course Trixie has always been secretive and no doubt she is delighted to be stealing a march on her cousin...'

Trixie opened her mouth and closed it again with a snap, and the professor, without looking at her, gave her hand a reassuring squeeze. 'I do not think that either of us thought about Margaret, indeed I do not quite see why we should have done so. I have to return to Holland for some weeks very shortly and Beatrice and I shall marry before we go. I am honoured that she has consented to be my wife...'

'But the wedding? How am I supposed to arrange a wedding in such a short time—bridesmaids and a reception and clothes?'

'We wish to marry very quietly—just the two of us.'

Aunt Alice looked relieved. 'Oh, well, in that case Margaret won't need to be a bridesmaid—it would upset her terribly, you know, Trixie getting married first. You will have no guests?'

'None, Mrs Doveton.'

'I must tell your uncle, Trixie, I don't know what he'll say,' and then belatedly, 'I'm sure I wish you both happy.' She rang the bell by the fireplace and when the maid came told her to ask the master to come to the drawing-room at once.

Uncle William, surprised though he was, was a good deal nicer about it than his wife had been. He kissed Trixie, wished her happy and shook the professor by the hand. 'I'm delighted to see you happily settled,' he told Trixie. 'You must come and see us when you come back from Holland—a small party for you—Trixie has a number of friends even though we see so little of her. Can't think why she doesn't come here more often.'

A remark which earned him a frown from his wife which the professor, standing between them, saw with amusement. It would, he reflected, give him great pleasure to bring Beatrice to dinner.

'So you cannot tell us the date of your wedding?' asked Aunt Alice.

'That isn't possible. It depends on my commitments both here and in Holland. You will agree with us that in the circumstances a quiet wedding which can take place quickly is the only answer.'

'Oh, well,' said Aunt Alice, 'it does seem the only solution. Do let us know when you are married.'

'Certainly, Mrs Doveton.' The professor smiled his charming smile, his eyes like blue flint. 'And now we mustn't keep you from your dinner party.' He looked down at Trixie, standing so quietly beside him. 'We also have our evening planned, have we not, my dear?'

She said, 'Yes,' as convincingly as possible, submitted to Aunt Alice's kiss somewhere near her cheek, kissed her uncle and watched the professor make his farewells, something which he did with easy good manners.

'Give my love to Margaret,' said Trixie as they left.

The last thing Mrs Doveton intended doing. 'On no account is Margaret to be told,' she admonished her husband. 'She will only have hysterics and young Mr Spence will be here shortly to take her to the ball. I will tell her tomorrow.'

Which she did, and was rewarded by Margaret having hysterics. 'The very idea!' she screamed. 'The scheming wretch, daring to get married before me, and to that man too—all that money and they say he's got a lovely house as well as a place in Holland. How did she do it? We've all tried to get him interested...he must be blind—she's so plain and dowdy.' She burst into fresh floods of tears and only stopped when her mother pointed out that she wouldn't be fit to be seen if she didn't pull herself together...

*　　*　　*

The professor and Trixie got back to the car and he said thoughtfully as he drove away, 'I do not like your aunt, Beatrice.'

'Well, I don't either, but she looked after me for years and sent me to the same school as Margaret and dressed me...'

'And loved you?'

'Well, no. But then I wasn't a real niece—Uncle William was Father's brother.'

'You would not mind if we saw rather little of them once we are married?'

'No. I thought you were splendid...'

'Thank you. Shall we have dinner somewhere? There are one or two details to settle.'

'That would be very nice, but I'm not dressed...'

He turned the car away from the heart of the city. 'We'll go to a delightful pub at Stonor—north of Henley. I've booked a table for half-past eight.'

He drove down to Brent and then on to the A40 and the M40, driving fast and silently until he turned off the motorway and took a country road to Stonor. The Stonor Arms was an eighteenth-century inn, skilfully converted, and the professor couldn't have chosen a better place to soothe Trixie's rather battered spirits. They had their drinks in a restful atmosphere and then dined in a leisurely fashion on terrine of duck, fish served with a samphire sauce, lamb cutlets and a fruit tart with lashings of cream. Throughout the meal the professor sustained a rambling conversation about nothing in particular, never mentioning Aunt Alice or Margaret or their own future, so that by the time they reached their coffee Trixie had become her usual matter-of-fact self again.

The professor, an observant man despite his absent-mindedness, eased the flow of inconsequential nothings.

'I shall be going to Holland in two weeks' time. If you are agreeable we will marry on the day of departure. You do not need to concern yourself with the arrangements to do with your leaving. I will attend to those. Have you any particular church in mind?'

'No. I don't think so. I go to St Ethelburga's—it's close to Timothy's.'

'Then we will be wed there.' He sat back, completely at ease. 'Let me see, if we marry in the forenoon we can get a ferry from Dover in the early afternoon and be in Leiden by the evening. I have to examine students on the following morning.'

It was daunting, to say the least. 'But will you want me there?' She did her best to sound sensible.

'Of course. I shall be there for three days; we shall stay at my home nearby.'

'Then after that?'

'We shall visit my parents and then go back to my home. I can arrange my consultations from there. I need to be back at Timothy's some time before Christmas. Are you agreeable to this?'

'Yes—yes. I don't need to see Aunt Alice again before we get married?'

'Only if you wish to. Is there any particular friend you would like to have at the church?'

She shook her head. 'I've several friends; if I asked one or two that wouldn't be fair on all the others.'

'A wise decision. Perhaps it might be a good idea to invite your friends and mine for drinks one evening when we return to London.'

'I thought you didn't like parties?'

'Nor do I, but I like my friends, and, well, I think they would expect something of that sort.' He smiled a little. 'Besides, when we have done our duty I will be left in peace to get on with my book.'

Trixie was beginning to hate that book. It was a great pity that she had to fall in love with a man so absorbed in his work that he paid no heed to the life going on around him, but, since she had, she would make the best of it. He wanted a buffer and she would be just that and somehow she would go through their life together without once allowing him to guess that she loved him.

He said suddenly, 'I sometimes wonder what you are thinking behind that quiet face, Beatrice.'

She smiled widely. 'Just at this moment I'm thinking that I ought to be getting back to Timothy's. I'm on duty in the morning and take-in week starts tomorrow.'

They left the pleasant place and started on their way back to town.

'How is your patient?' she wanted to know. 'The private patient with exophthalmos.'

'Doing well, I'm glad to say. She presents a most interesting picture—I was expecting corneal ulceration at the very least but there is little sign of that. Now, I have another patient on the wards—an euthyroid case with entirely different symptoms...'

He enlarged upon them for the rest of the journey and Trixie, quite content to listen to his voice, didn't really hear a word of what he was telling her; indeed, she thought it likely that he had forgotten her for the moment. As they neared the hospital he observed, 'A pleasant evening, Beatrice. You are a most satisfactory companion. You are not unhappy about your aunt and uncle? I am very willing for them to come to our wedding if you wish that.'

'I don't, thank you. I think that the less they know about it the better it will be for everyone. Margaret is sure to be—well, upset. She has always expected to marry and she will feel that I've behaved badly, so they won't want to know anything about it, if you see what I mean.'

The professor said with a trace of impatience, 'Yes, yes, of course. I believe I will see your matron in the morning and arrange things with her. Do you wish to continue working until we marry or shall I find somewhere for you to stay?'

'I'd rather work...'

'Very well. We shall probably see very little of each other—I have to go to Birmingham within the next day or so and I have a number of private patients to attend as well as a couple of consultations at Bristol. I'll let you know the details later on.'

He had stopped the car before the hospital entrance and got out to open her door. 'I almost forgot; don't bring a lot of clothes with you, just enough for a few days—you can shop in the Hague.'

He patted her on the shoulder in a big-brotherly fashion and bade her goodnight and opened the entrance door for her. His manners were beyond reproach.

He had been right; she saw almost nothing of him during the next two weeks. For a good deal of that time he was away, and although he came on to the ward from time to time he allowed himself no more than a small smile if their glances met.

She had been sent for to the office and had listened to Matron explaining that she might leave since the circumstances were unusual, adding the corollary that Trixie must try and live up to the life expected of her. 'Professor van der Brink-Schaaksma is a famous man in his particular sphere,' she was told, 'both in this country and in Europe, indeed he has been called to consultations in various parts of the world. I understand him to own a charming house in Holland. I hope you will be happy, Nurse Doveton.' She sound doubtful.

Trixie had told Lucy and asked her not to breathe a word to anyone for the moment, a needless precaution for a patient had excitedly pointed out the notice of their engagement in the *Telegraph* and in no time at all the entire hospital had the news.

Trixie was well liked—with the exception of Staff Nurse Bennett, of course—and congratulations were sincere if surprised.

'How on earth did you manage it?' asked Mary in her blighting manner. 'I should have thought you were the very last girl the professor would fall for.'

Which, Trixie had to admit to herself, was probably perfectly true. She only smiled kindly at the girl and pointed out that there was no accounting for tastes. Mary had to have her spiteful say.

'At least he won't be distracted from his work by your pretty face.'

'Now why didn't I think of that?' asked Trixie composedly. 'I dare say that would be as good a reason as any for getting married to a plain girl.'

Indeed, when she thought about it, it was the very reason why the professor had asked her to marry him. There were other reasons too of course: guarding his precious spare time and his privacy, being a hostess when needed. She could think of half a dozen—she only hoped that she would be able to deal with them all in a manner to please him.

'Time will tell,' she muttered, her head in her clothes cupboard, wondering what to throw out and what to keep. The pile of discarded clothes got larger and larger until there was barely enough to cover her decently. Days off, she thought happily; she would spend them both shopping. There wasn't much money in her bank account but she intended to spend it. The professor had always been polite about her clothes, but there was such a thing as damning with faint praise...

A velvet suit, she decided, and never mind a sensible winter coat—it was mild weather for November and although he had never mentioned his intentions she supposed that he would give her enough money to buy clothes suitable to their way of life. So she spent a morning looking for what she wanted, and found it: sapphire-blue velvet, a neat jacket and a slim skirt, not too short. She had nice legs but she wasn't sure of the professor's views on the subject of legs. She found a silk blouse to go with it, shoes, gloves and handbag, and, since it was her wedding, a pretty little hat with a sideways tilt to its small brim which made her face rather more interesting. It was wonderful what clothes did for one, she reflected, pirouetting before the enormous looking-glass in the hat shop. She had spent a good deal of money; separates from Marks and Spencer, more blouses, a couple of woollies and undies took care of what was left. She went back to Timothy's with an empty purse, consoling herself with the thought that she would have part of her month's salary to collect when she left.

There had been nothing from her aunt and uncle, but then, she reminded herself, they didn't know the date of the wedding. She hadn't known it herself until she had had a terse note from the professor. It had been hard to read his fearful scrawl but the PS was clearer. He would be in the entrance hall on the evening before the wedding and hoped that she would dine with him so that any problems might be discussed.

Saying goodbye was a wrench; she had been happy at Timothy's and even Sister Snell expressed the hope that

she would be happy, but it was left to the patients to
shake her hand and kiss her and make small offerings
of lawn hankies and lavender bags. She went to her room
and brooded over her wardrobe. She had nothing to
wear. It would actually have to be the jersey again and
her winter coat, but once in the jersey she decided that
it just wouldn't do, it would have to be the blue crêpe
again. Which meant that she was five minutes late in
reaching the entrance hall.

She skimmed across its vastness, a little out of breath.
'Hello—I'm sorry I'm late.'

'Don't apologise; in any case I have any number of
things to think about.'

'Patients?'

'Yes. I think that I shall have to fly over in a few days'
time to check on their progress.'

'Will you have time to see them tomorrow?'

He stared down at her earnest face. 'Our wedding day?
Is that not an insult to the bride, Beatrice?'

'I'm not that kind of bride, am I? And it will only
take a short time to get married.'

'You are a most understanding girl. There will be time
after we have had lunch—I could call in on our way to
the ferry.' His blue eyes searched her face. 'You do not
mind?'

'Not a bit,' she lied stoutly, and was rewarded by a
kiss on her cheek, something which Murgatroyd watched
with sentimental pleasure. A nice pair of love-birds, he
thought erroneously.

He took her to his house for dinner and Mies welcomed her with a delighted twinkle. 'All is prepared,'
she told them as they went in. 'There is champagne on
ice and a dinner of such splendour that I have prepared.'

Indeed it was splendid: crab bisque, not out of a tin, breast of chicken in a wine and cream sauce with tiny sprouts, potato balls and baby carrots and lastly a pavlova with fresh pineapple and whipped cream. They ate leisurely and the talk was casual and unforced. It was at the end of the meal that the professor said suddenly, 'I knew that I had forgotten something; I did remember it some days ago but it slipped my memory.'

He fished around in a pocket and took out a small jeweller's box.

'The family engagement ring—it is handed on from one bride to the next. It is very old and it is usual for the men in the family to give a ring of their own choosing at the same time. I must see about that...in the meantime, will you wear this?'

It was a sapphire with diamonds on either side of it mounted plainly in gold. Very beautiful, as beautiful as on the day the first bride had had it put on her finger by the man who loved her. The professor handed her the box and she put the ring on herself and wondered while she was doing it to whom it would go next. There were to be no children, she supposed, for she was to be a wife in name only. She swallowed back sudden tears and thanked him quietly.

He drove her back presently and went into the hospital with her. Some notes he had left on the ward, he explained, bidding her goodnight in his kind voice, but she could see that his thoughts weren't with her any more. She said brightly, 'See you tomorrow, Krijn,' and nipped smartly through the door to the nurses' home and up to her room where she found her numerous friends gathered.

'A farewell party,' they told her gleefully, and produced sherry, and potato crisps, and sat around talking until an indignant warden stalked in to know why the lights weren't out and did they knew it was almost midnight? When everyone had gone Trixie got into bed, and, against all her expectations, went to sleep at once.

CHAPTER FOUR

TRIXIE woke early, jumped out of bed and went to look out of the window. It was still dark and the street-lamps cast their fierce orange glow over the surrounding roofs and chimney-pots, glistening with a light frost. At least it wasn't raining. There was no point in getting back into bed. She crept soundlessly along to the kitchen and made herself some tea and was still there drinking it when the night nurse came to wake the day nurses.

'Aren't you wildly excited?' she asked, accepting the last of the tea.

'Yes,' said Trixie, and reflected that she was scared too. Supposing it didn't work out? It had all seemed so sensible when the professor had first broached the subject of their marriage; now in the light of a November morning the whole thing was ridiculous. She could, of course, telephone his house and tell him that she had changed her mind, but that wouldn't do—she had agreed to marry him, and besides, she loved him.

She pottered around, bidding her friends goodbye once more, watching them going down to their breakfasts with a pang of uncertainty about her future, but once the home was quiet she had a bath, ate some of the breakfast which had been sent over, and got dressed. They were to be married at ten o'clock and she would be fetched, the professor had told her, at a quarter to the hour. She felt better when she was ready; the new outfit suited her and the little hat sat nicely on her mousy hair. She checked her case, closed it and went through her handbag once more: passport, powder and lipstick, hanky, cheque-book and money, and sat down on her bed. There was still a little time before she needed to go down and she found herself wishing that Aunt Alice or Uncle William would telephone—just to wish her happiness. She had written them a note telling them the date and the time of the wedding, knowing that they wouldn't come to the church, but hoping that they would have wished her well. She sighed, looked at her watch again and saw that it was time to go.

Colonel Vosper was in the hall. 'I hope you will give me the pleasure of giving you away, my dear,' he greeted her. 'Krijn agreed with me that it would be a most fitting thing to do. I have known him for years, you know, and I couldn't wish for a more charming bride for him.'

Trixie had a sudden wish to burst into tears, but she didn't know why. She smiled widely instead. 'Oh, how very nice, I can't think of anything I should like better.' She leaned up and kissed his old cheek and took his arm, and they went out of the hospital and got into his car and drove to the church.

It was a small church, a thing of dignity and ancient beauty amid its shabby surroundings. Inside someone had arranged flowers; chrysanthemums and freesias and carnations and roses. There was a posy on the porch seat too, lilies of the valley and violets and rosebuds. She walked down the short aisle on the colonel's arm, her small nose sniffing appreciatively at their scent, her eyes on the professor's vast person, standing quite at ease, talking to the vicar. Mies was there too, turning to smile at her from under a sensible hat. Trixie would have liked Krijn to have turned and smiled at her too but he didn't; she reached his side and peeped up at his calm face. He smiled at her then. She had seen him smile like that so many times at a nervous patient: kindly and impersonal.

It didn't take long to get married. They bade the vicar goodbye and went out to the two cars and this time the colonel took Mies with him and Trixie got in beside Krijn. The colonel drove off first and by the time the professor drew up before his own front door Mies was there to open it, and when they went into the drawing-room the colonel had a bottle of champagne in his hands. He opened it at once and toasted the bride and groom, complimented Trixie on her charming appearance, told the professor what a lucky chap he was and added, 'I suppose the honeymoon is a secret?'

'We'll send you a postcard,' said Trixie quickly, because Krijn, just for a brief moment, had looked taken aback; she suspected that a honeymoon hadn't been among his plans.

They went into lunch presently: smoked salmon, lobster thermidor with a winter salad and, for a dessert, a wedding cake. Mies carried it in proudly. 'This I make myself,' she declared triumphantly, 'my present to you, madam, and you, Professor.'

'Mies, how wonderful!' exclaimed Trixie. 'Thank you very much. Krijn, isn't it a marvellous present? We have to cut it together. Mies, you must stay and have a slice, and Gladys too, if you would fetch her.'

The professor had hidden his surprise very well. He said something to Mies in Dutch and she laughed happily before going to fetch the maid, and the colonel said cheerfully, 'I say, what a splendid idea—she's a treasure, your housekeeper.' He gave a chuckle. 'Makes you feel married, doesn't it? You have to save some for the first christening, you know.' He chuckled again at Trixie's pink cheeks.

The little party broke up soon afterwards and they were seen off by the colonel and Mies, waving goodbye from the doorstep, and in the car Trixie said, 'What a delightful wedding, and thank you for the lovely flowers, Krijn, they were really beautiful.'

'Flowers? Ah, yes, of course. I'm glad you liked them,' and she settled back in her seat, happy at his thoughtfulness, unaware that it had been Mies who had reminded him that flowers were absolutely obligatory at a wedding and what about a bouquet for his bride? He had looked up from the book he was reading and told her in an absent-minded manner to do what she thought was the right thing and then he had gone back to his studying and forgotten all about it.

He drove to Timothy's and parked the car in the consultant's bay. 'Would you rather come inside and wait?' he asked. 'I don't expect to be very long.'

'Then I'll stay here,' said Trixie cheerfully, and watched him cross the forecourt to the entrance. She studied his back with loving eyes; he really was a very large man and he dressed with a quiet elegance. She wondered if he would turn round when he reached the door but he didn't.

She sat quietly for ten minutes or so and then reached for the set of maps in the pocket on the door beside her. There was a large map of Holland; she unfolded it and studied it carefully. There were a great many villages dotted round Leiden; it had been silly of her not to have asked the name of Krijn's home. Some of the names looked strange; she supposed that she would have to learn Dutch if they were to live for a good deal of the time in Holland. She conned the map, picking out the larger towns; Holland was a country she knew almost nothing about. It would be a good idea to get to know something about it, and what better than a map?

By the time Krijn came back she knew quite a lot about Holland, and she also longed for a cup of tea. If she hadn't been so much in love with him, she might have felt peevish at the sight of him, at last, coming slowly from the entrance, his registrar on one side, Dr Johnson on the other. They were deep in conversation and it was obvious to her that he had quite forgotten that she had been sitting there for more than an hour and that there was a ferry to catch. For fear that he might look up and see her watching him, she looked out of the other window.

Her door was opened and the three men stood there. Dr Johnson and the registrar beaming and offering congratulations and the professor looking at her with a kind of astonished concern.

'Beatrice, I am sorry that I have been so much longer than I expected. Something turned up...'

She smiled forgiveness, foreseeing any number of occasions in the future when something would turn up. She would get used to that in time, of course.

They would have to drive fast to catch the ferry from Dover. They were still in the heart of the city, caught in the start of the rush-hour, when he reached for the phone.

'Mrs Grey? Cancel our booking on the ferry, will you? We can't make it. Get me a place on the next one, please. There should be one later.' He listened for a moment. 'Good. Do that—thanks... The least I can offer in apology is tea, Beatrice. We will stop in Bexley.'

'Won't we miss the ferry...? But you cancelled it, didn't you?'

'Yes, but we can sail on the following one. We shall be an hour or two later home, that is all.'

He stopped the car in Bexley, outside a small cosy-looking café, and they had tea and toast and presently drove on again, in time to go aboard an almost empty ship. The crossing took over three hours and they had dinner on board before disembarking at Ostend. Within a short time they had crossed into Holland at Sluis, caught the ferry at Breskens, and, once in Vlissingen, took the motorway. Trixie was tired by now; the road stretched ahead of them, running through flat polder land, glimpsed in the car's powerful headlamps. She had no idea where they were; the motorway circumvented the towns and the villages. She was surprised when Krijn told her that they had only a few more miles to go.

It was very dark by now, and, although the car was warm, she thought that it might be unpleasantly chilly outside. There was a glow in the sky ahead of them and the professor said, 'Leiden—we're almost there. We'll go straight home...'

She murmured thankfully. She was tired, dying for a cup of tea and faintly scared. If he had suggested that he should call in at some hospital or other she would have been unable to prevent herself from screaming.

They were still on the motorway; the professor had ignored several turn-offs to Leiden and the cup of tea seemed further away than ever, but her spirits rose when he turned off on to a narrow brick road away from the city, driving into its darkness with the confidence of someone who knew exactly where he was going. Presently she saw the faint gleam of water and then a scattering of small houses on either side of the road. It was still dark with barely a glimmer of light coming from their windows. He slowed through a small village with a looming church and turned into a smooth drive, past tall brick pillars. The drive wound through shrubs and trees to make a final twist before the house. Krijn slid to a smooth halt before its majestic door and got out to open Trixie's door. 'Home,' he said briefly, took her arm and marched her across the sweep to the door now open. She barely had time to take in the solid grandeur of the house, four square, with its rows of large windows, most of them gleaming with light, before she was urged inside into a lobby, the inner door open on to the square hall beyond. There was a middle-aged, rather stout man holding the door, who replied with a dignified pleasure to the professor's clap on the back, and, when introduced as Rabo the butler, shook her hand and bowed slightly, at the same time making a welcoming speech in heavily accented English. Trixie, much heartened by his obvious sincerity, beamed at him. 'You speak English— oh, how glad I am—I was a bit worried, you know...'

'It will be my pleasure to help you in any way possible, *mevrouw*,' said Rabo. 'You will find us all wishing to do all we can...'

The professor had thrown his coat on to a chair and turned to speak to a tall sturdy woman. 'Wolke...' He shook her hand and spoke in his own language before putting out an arm to draw Trixie to him. 'Trixie, this is Wolke, my housekeeper and Rabo's wife. She speaks a little English, but she understands quite a lot. She will take you upstairs to your room; you must want to tidy yourself.' A remark which annoyed her very much, although she forgot the annoyance when he added, 'Come down again as soon as you can. We will have coffee and sandwiches in the drawing-room while I tell you a little about my plans.'

So she followed Wolke's imposing figure up the gracefully curving staircase at the back of the hall and crossed the gallery above it to enter the room the housekeeper was indicating. It was a beautiful room, furnished splendidly with a four-poster bed and delicate mahogany dressing-table, bedside tables and several extremely comfortable chairs. There was a day bed underneath the two long windows and several lamps here and there, shaded in peach-pink, casting a welcoming glow. Wolke crossed the room and opened a door, revealing a bathroom, nodding and smiling rather like a magician who had carried off a trick satisfactorily before sliding more doors open on to a vast expanse of cupboard, fitted with rails and drawers and shelves, which, Trixie decided, would take her a lifetime to fill.

Left alone, she inspected herself in the pier-glass; she didn't need tidying at all. At the same time she washed her face and hands, powdered her small nose, combed her hair to even greater smoothness and went downstairs again. Rabo was hovering in the hall and led her to great double doors on one side of it which he flung open with something of a flourish.

She went past him with a little smile of thanks, concealing shyness at the prospect of sitting opposite Krijn in what was now her home. She was greeted by a low rumble as a Great Dane loped across the room to her; the rumble sounded welcoming when the professor got up from his chair by the fire with a quiet, 'Your missus, Samson; say hello.'

Trixie stood still while the big dog offered a head for a gentle scratch and Krijn strolled over to her. 'You like dogs? I should have asked...'

'I like them very much—cats too. He's a beauty, isn't he?'

'Indeed, yes. Come over to the fire. Rabo is just bringing coffee. It's late but you can sleep the clock round if you wish.'

She sat down opposite him and saw a pile of letters on the table beside his chair. 'Please read your letters,' she begged him. 'I'm quite happy just to sit. I didn't expect this.' She waved a small, nicely kept hand around her. 'It's rather grand, isn't it?'

He smiled a little. 'It's your home, Beatrice. You're sure you don't mind if I go through these?'

She sat quietly, exploring the room with her eyes. Later, she promised herself, when she was alone, she would go over it by the inch. It was beautiful, full of treasures and yet lived-in. Her slow survey was interrupted by Rabo's entrance with a tray of coffee and sandwiches. She poured from a gleaming silver coffee-pot, still in use after what she guessed might be a couple of hundred years. The coffee-cups must have been almost as old; biscuit china fluted and gilt-edged. The sandwiches were up-to-date: smoked salmon, ham cut wafer-thin, chicken and egg and cress. Trixie sank her excellent teeth into the salmon and Krijn put down his coffee-cup and said, 'Ah, yes—we must have a little talk...'

The telephone on the table beside him rang in a muted way and he picked up the receiver. Whoever it was made him smile as he listened before answering in his own language. He glanced at his watch as he put the receiver down.

'They knew that I would be here some time this evening,' he told Trixie, 'at the hospital in Leiden. There's a case—they would like me to see it in the morning first thing. You'll be all right here? Make yourself at home—unpack—Wolke will be delighted to take you round. I'll come home for lunch.' He smiled at her kindly. 'You must be very tired?'

If that wasn't a broad hint to take herself off to bed, she was a Dutchman—no, a Dutchwoman now that she was married—and unpacking would take her all of ten minutes. She would have liked another sandwich—several—but he was frowning over a letter. Hurriedly she got to her feet, and he glanced up and said, 'Off to bed? I dare say you are tired.' He went to the doors with her and opened them, putting a hand on her shoulder. 'I hope you will be happy here, Beatrice. You have only to ask Rabo if you want anything.' He smiled at her. 'We must have a little talk...goodnight.'

She bade him goodnight and went up the staircase; he had a beautiful manner, but he had a letter in his hand she sensed he was wanting to read, so that she had refrained from any comment about the day. He had probably, she thought sadly, quite forgotten that they had got married that morning.

She undressed slowly, had a long, blissfully hot bath, and got into bed. She supposed that she wouldn't see him until he returned at lunchtime when, hopefully, they could have the little talk. The bed was delightfully soft and warm and she had had an exciting day. She closed her eyes and sensibly went to sleep.

She woke to find a girl, very neat in a cotton dress, beaming at her from the side of the bed. She held a small tray of tea which she put down on a bedside table, nodding and smiling before going over to the window and drawing back the long silk curtains. It was raining from a grey sky but the girl waved an arm at the view, nodded several times and went away.

Trixie drank her tea and went to have a look out of the windows. She was at the front of the house, overlooking a stretch of lawn and flower-beds which in summer must present a glorious sight. The sweep before the door was directly below her and she could see the drive to one side of it.

There were trees everywhere and a glimpse of open country beyond. She had a sudden happy urge to explore, and, showered and dressed in Marks and Spencer, she went downstairs. Rabo must have been on the lookout for her, for he appeared at the foot of the stairs with a fatherly good morning and the advice that breakfast was waiting for her.

She followed him into a small room behind the drawing-room, where a small round table had been laid before a bright fire, and sat down at it. The coffee smelled delicious, and there was toast and boiled eggs and honey. She breathed a sigh of pleasure; never mind the grey morning outside, inside was everything anyone could wish for...

Wolke, Rabo told her, would be honoured to take her round the house whenever she wished—she had only to say.

'I'd like that, Rabo. Would after I've had breakfast suit Wolke?'

He inclined his head. 'Of course, *mevrouw*. Is there anything else you would like?'

When she said no, he slid away, leaving her to make a good breakfast and wonder about the day ahead of her.

The inspection of the house took a good deal of the morning; as well as the drawing-room and the small room where she had had her breakfast there was a dining-room, very formal, with finely panelled walls and a massive table surrounded by a dozen chairs, a vast sideboard and a great many rather dark paintings arranged upon its dark red damask walls. On the other side of the hall there was a library, its walls lined with books, a few comfortable chairs arranged invitingly around small tables. Beyond that was the professor's study. She didn't go in there, only stood at the door, imagining him sitting at the solid desk, concentrating on his books...

Upstairs she lost count of the rooms leading from the gallery and on the flight above there were still more rooms, all furnished with great good taste, and on one side of the circular landing there was a baize door opening on to the nursery wing, which was light and airy with enough space to take half a dozen children. Trixie caught Wolke's knowing eye and blushed under her motherly beam, and tried not to think of the small Krijns she was doubtful she would ever see there.

There was another floor where Rabo and Wolke and two maids had their rooms under the curved roof where there was a series of attics. They led on to the tiles, but when Trixie would have explored further Wolke said firmly, 'It is time for your coffee, *mevrouw*,' so they went back downstairs and she drank her coffee in the drawing-room in the company of a very ordinary cat. There was no sign of Samson and when she asked Rabo he told her that the dog went everywhere with his master and would return with him presently. He added with a benign smile, 'If *mevrouw* wishes the cat to be removed...?'

'Oh, no. I like cats. What is his name?'

'Percy, *mevrouw*. He is company for Samson.' Rabo took himself off with smooth silence and Trixie drank her coffee, and, since it had left off raining, went upstairs and got her sensible shoes and raincoat, tied her head in a scarf and went looking for a side-door. Rabo, she decided, must have second sight or something; he materialised beside her, offered to show her a small door at the end of a little passage beside the staircase and mentioned that the door from the conservatory at the back of the house was always open during the day. 'Lunch is at half-past twelve,' he told her, 'and if I might suggest, *mevrouw*, you should remain within the grounds. The professor will take you walking and down to the village so that you may know your way around.' He glanced out at the sodden landscape. 'The country hereabouts is very pretty.'

The house stood in large grounds, sheltered by trees and surrounded by a high brick wall. Trixie was poking around a small summerhouse built into the wall some way from the house when she was startled by Krijn's voice.

'You are finding your way around?' he wanted to know. 'Not the best of days in which to see Holland for the first time. You have been round the house?'

'Yes. It is beautiful and very large. Has it always been your home?'

He was leaning against a crooked apple tree. 'Yes— I was born here. My parents moved to Friesland when my grandfather died—the house there goes from father to son, and the eldest son takes over here until such time as it is his turn to take his father's place. You see, the family comes from Friesland but a long time ago an eldest son came to Leiden to study medicine and this house was built for him.'

'Have all your ancestors been medical men?'

'Yes—it must be a hereditary urge.'

They began to walk back to the house and Samson moved silently to join them from the trees.

'Did the students do well?' she asked.

'On the whole, yes. I had to fail half a dozen. They're qualified men wanting to specialise...'

'Oh, I see. Will you be here this afternoon?'

'I have a consultation at three o'clock. You can come into Leiden if you wish—you must want to do some shopping?'

He must have noticed her one suitcase and small overnight bag. 'Well, I haven't much with me—you said only bring enough for a few days...'

'Indeed I did. Have you money, Beatrice?'

She did some quick reckoning. 'Is there a Marks and Spencer in Leiden—or something similar?'

'I think not. Wolke would know. There is a branch in Rotterdam. Why do you wish to go there?' He stopped to look down at her. 'How much money do you have, Beatrice?'

His eyebrows rose when she told him. 'But my dear girl, that is barely sufficient to buy you a pair of shoes.'

There didn't seem any point in telling him that she could have bought shoes and some sort of sensible coat or jacket and had enough over to look for a blouse.

'You will, of course, have an allowance now that you are my wife,' said the professor. 'I'll see about it this afternoon. In the meantime I suggest that I take you to the Hague tomorrow so that you can buy whatever you need.'

His rather sleepy eyes studied her sensible skirt and sweater. 'You always look nice,' he told her—a remark she didn't quite believe but it was comforting to hear anyway, 'but you will need the kind of clothes women wear in the evening—I have friends and colleagues here and their wives will want to meet you—tea parties and so forth.'

Trixie looked down at her sensible shoes, the warm colour flooding her cheeks. He was ashamed of her...she swallowed sudden rage.

'Don't be angry,' said the professor, putting a finger unerringly on the crux of the matter. 'You had no reason to wear haute couture when you were nursing but now you will have to dress the part, I'm afraid. I shall enjoy feeling proud of you.'

'Don't butter me up,' she muttered crossly and glared up at him.

When he laughed gently she forgot her hurt feelings and laughed too, and he said, 'That's better. We shall have a splendid day shopping. It is not my forte, I'm afraid, and after tomorrow I dare say you will have to shop by yourself.'

'You don't need to come.'

'Oh, but I do, otherwise I shall worry in case you have gone to Marks and Spencer in Rotterdam.'

They had reached the house and went indoors to eat their lunch in a pleasant comradeship. Trixie, sitting opposite him in the grandeur of the dining-room, eyed him lovingly and thought that he probably treated his four sisters exactly as he was treating her. It was a depressing thought, but the truth, she reminded herself, wasn't always palatable.

They had their coffee at the table while he explained that he would fetch her the following day some time after one o'clock. 'I'm examining in the morning, but I should be free by then. It is only a few miles to den Haag, so you will have three or four hours to shop. I'm sure you will need longer than that—my sisters have made that plain to me on several occasions—but I'll show you where the best shops are and you may have time to get one or two things.' He passed his cup for more coffee. 'I shall be examining again on the following morning;

if we leave a little earlier I can take you to den Haag
before I start work.' He frowned in thought. 'I'll arrange to pick you up about three o'clock. I'll show you
where tomorrow.'

She tried not to feel disappointment when he observed presently that he would be in his study if she
wanted him. 'An excellent opportunity to correct some
notes,' he told her. She had no doubt at all that as he
went through the door he had forgotten her, his brilliant
brain already dealing with some tricky gland or other.
Samson went with him, and, left alone, she wandered
into the library, found a book and settled in one of the
comfortable chairs, but she didn't read—there was a pad
on the table at her elbow and a pen beside it. She began
to make a list of all the clothes she thought might be
required by an eminent consultant's wife. It was a long
list but he had said that she would have to dress the part.
She added a second jersey outfit and some sort of wrap
for the evening. She would have liked one of those dramatic ones actresses in soap operas flung so negligently
over one shoulder, but she wasn't tall enough, and besides she wasn't sure if she could fling with sufficient
drama. A sensible mohair stole, perhaps, or a little velvet
jacket? She brooded happily until Rabo came to tell her
that he would be serving tea in the drawing-room.

Krijn was already there, reading a newspaper with
Samson beside him. He got up as she went in, begged
her to pour out and asked her if she had enjoyed her
afternoon.

'Oh, very much. I made a list of clothes. It's a very
long one...'

'In that case two days' shopping won't suffice. When
we come back from Friesland you must persevere until
the list is dealt with.'

'If you don't mind me asking,' said Trixie in her sensible way, 'don't you mind how much I spend?'

'No, within reasonable limits, of course.'

'Yes, but I think that your reasonable limits and mine aren't the same.'

'Well, since you are so anxious, shall we say...?' He mentioned a sum which made her gape.

'You can't mean that; it's a fortune!'

'Nevertheless that is the amount at your disposal, Beatrice.' He spoke pleasantly, but she detected a trace of impatience in his voice and it was perhaps fortunate that the phone rang at that moment and he became absorbed in a long conversation. When he finally put the phone down it was to say that he was going to the hospital.

Rather late in the day for another consultation, reflected Trixie, receiving the news with what she hoped was wifely compliance; it must be a patient.

She changed into the brown velvet later and went back to the drawing-room to sit by the fire. Tomorrow, she promised herself, she would get some wool or embroidery of some kind. The newspaper lay where he had discarded it, and she picked it up. Of course she couldn't understand a word; the sooner she got herself a dictionary, and preferably someone to teach her the language, the quicker she would feel at home. She thought fleetingly of her aunt and uncle and her friends at Timothy's and was surprised that she felt no regret at leaving them. She would have to make new friends in Holland, and, hopefully, Krijn's family would accept her. Over and above that, she had him. She didn't mind about anything else.

At half-past seven Rabo came to ask her if the professor had told her that he would be late for dinner, and she had to confess that he hadn't mentioned that at all, only said that he would have to go to the hospital.

'The professor,' said Rabo with faintly critical dignity, 'is at times absent-minded.'

Trixie agreed. 'Can Wolke keep dinner back for a while?' she asked.

'The soup will not spoil, *mevrouw*, and the sweet is a creme caramel which will not spoil either.' He didn't mention what came in between; something which would be ruined, no doubt.

'Well, could you ask her to wait a little longer, please? I'm sure the professor will return as soon as he is able to.'

Words she would have choked upon if she could have seen him at that moment, sitting in the consultant's room, deep in a most interesting discussion about someone's adrenal glands, quite oblivious of the time.

It was gone half-past eight when he came in and found her sitting by the fire. 'Ah, there you are,' he remarked and then stopped short. 'Good lord, is that the time? I had a most interesting case and quite overlooked dinner. You've had yours?'

'No,' said Trixie and felt goaded into adding, 'You see, I had no idea when you would be back.'

He said with perfect good humour, 'I have allowed myself to become absent-minded. My apologies. I expect Wolke has salvaged something fit for us to eat.'

He poured her a glass of sherry, oblivious of her coolness, then sat down opposite to her to drink his Jenever. 'This patient I've been seeing,' he began, 'a most interesting case, I shall most certainly give a detailed account of it. I have the notes with me; I must write them up this evening.'

He smiled at her, an impersonal friendly smile which did nothing to improve her feelings. 'I promise you I'll keep to our plans for tomorrow. After lunch, wasn't it? It is the last of the exams in the morning; we will go to Friesland in two days' time—I can spare a day or two.'

Rabo announced dinner and they sat down to soup, an elaborate dish of chicken coated in a delicious sauce— a successful effort on Wolke's part to transform the chicken à la king into something edible—and the creme caramel. The meal was a pleasant one, but the professor showed no urge to sit over it. After a suitable interval in the drawing-room over the coffee-cups he excused himself, wishing her a friendly goodnight as he went.

Trixie went upstairs herself very shortly afterwards. If she spent any more time alone in this lovely room with no one for company save the occasional visit from Samson she would burst into tears.

She was tired, she told herself, getting ready for bed; things would get better. She blew her nose resolutely and forced her thoughts to dwell upon the shopping she would enjoy on the morrow.

CHAPTER FIVE

TRIXIE spent the next morning looking in cupboards with Wolke. It was apparent to her that was what she was expected to do, and the sooner she learnt to be a Dutch housewife the better. She ate a solitary lunch with Percy for company, and was ready and waiting by the time the professor arrived home. She had been pleasantly surprised to see him and had steeled herself to accept his late arrival, or no arrival at all, with the British phlegm so often attributed to her fellow countrywomen, so that her welcoming smile was warm enough for him to look twice at her.

She was wearing the tweed suit and one of the new blouses, and, since she hadn't a suitable hat, she was bareheaded. Not a suitable outfit for the professor's wife, she felt, but the best that she could do. She consoled herself with the thought that he wouldn't pay attention to her appearance anyway. Happily for her peace of mind, she was unaware that his sleepy eyes had taken in every smallest detail of her appearance.

He parked the car in the hospital forecourt and walked her to an arcade of shops—boutiques displaying one or two enticing outfits flung over little gilt chairs with studied carelessness.

'Your list,' he prompted her, standing patiently while she browsed to and fro. 'Something to wear when we go to Friesland? A dress or two...'

Two hours later they made their way back to the car, the professor carrying a number of large boxes and large plastic bags and Trixie, still gulping down the shock of spending so much money in such a short time, trotting beside him, the possessor of a winter coat of unsurpassed elegance, a new and very smart suit, a clutch of blouses, all of pure silk and costing, in her estimation, a small fortune, a jersey two-piece in the very latest style and two quite ravishing dresses which the professor had described as 'something informal for the evening'. She had paraded in front of him in first one and then the other and wondered what on earth he must have thought of the brown velvet.

He deposited his parcels in the boot and said, 'Tea, I think, don't you?' and walked her back to Lange Voorhout where they had tea at Des Indes Hotel. Over the dainty sandwiches and rich cream cakes he advised her to shop again on the following day. 'There must be quite a lot more,' he pointed out, 'and probably you will prefer to be on your own. I've arranged with the bank; I've a cheque-book for you and remind me to let you have some money for the small stuff.'

Trixie thanked him rather faintly. She was drunk with the delight of owning the kind of clothes she had until now admired in expensive shop windows. She said now, 'Thank you very much, Krijn, they'll last me ages—the things we bought today.'

He looked surprised. 'Beatrice, I do not expect you to wear your clothes threadbare; you will have an allowance and when you see something you would like to have, you will buy it.'

'Will I?' She added, 'I might be very extravagant; can you afford that?'

'I believe so. You are a sensible young woman, Beatrice, I do not expect you to bankrupt me.' He had spoken kindly but with a hint of impatience, so that she made haste to ask him if he still had examinations on the following day.

'No, only a lecture and a few patients whom I usually like to check up on when I come to Leiden. We will leave for Friesland on the day after tomorrow after breakfast and spend two days with my parents. When we get back I must keep some appointments already made for me and there will be clinics. I may possibly go to Brussels and Paris for brief visits. You will be quite happy here?' He smiled suddenly. 'I assume that you will be quite occupied; people will call and I rely upon you to think up good excuses for refusing too many invitations. There are some which are unavoidable but since we are newly married it shouldn't be too hard to plead a wish for privacy—isn't that what is expected of us? I'm sure you will know what to say. I do not need to go back to London for several weeks and in that time I shall be able to work quietly at home.'

She would get a lot of knitting done. Perhaps it would be more sensible to work a set of tapestry seats for the dining-room chairs; that should keep her nicely occupied. She swallowed resentment at his single-mindedness of purpose; she had known about that when she agreed to marry him and he had made it clear at the time, hadn't he—that she was to be his buffer? He was keeping to his side of their bargain, making sure that she had all she wanted and more, offering her a friendship which was better than nothing at all, and might indeed turn into something warmer given time.

'I'll do my best,' she assured him. 'It would help if you could spare time to write a list of your close friends...'

They went back home then to part in the hall, she to go to her room with her parcels and boxes, he to his study.

There was time to really try on and look at everything she had bought before dinner. She wore the simplest of the dresses—a patterned jersey silk which made the most of her pretty figure and was worth every penny of its price. Studying herself in the pier-glass she was moderately satisfied with her appearance; she would never be beautiful but perhaps with the aid of beautiful clothes she might achieve a kind of prettiness. She went downstairs carefully because she was wearing a pair of high-heeled shoes and went into the drawing-room smiling with the anticipation of Krijn's approval.

He got up as she went in and said cheerfully, 'Come and sit by the fire—the evenings are getting chilly. Have you been inspecting your purchases? I dare say you are looking forward to wearing them.'

He gave her a drink and went back to his chair and began to talk about the life she could expect to lead in Leiden. 'We are only a few miles from the town,' he observed, 'although there is no bus from the village—it's too small. You must explore it one day. I'm sure everyone is curious to meet you. Like all villages, the people in it know more about me than I do myself. Although we are so near Leiden it is a very quiet community—the young ones go to work, of course, but the older ones are content to work for the farmers around the village.'

She was a good listener, making the right remark at the right moment while she reflected that she might just as well have cut a hole in a bath towel and stuck her head through it. It was a great pity that he never really looked at her. That was one of the first things she must work on—of course he knew what she looked like, even noticed what she was wearing occasionally, but he never actually saw her.

They dined in the friendliest possible fashion but directly they had had their coffee in the drawing-room he excused himself and went to his study. It seemed unlikely that he would return and he didn't; Rabo had come to fetch Percy to his cushion in the kitchen and Samson was with his master. She decided to go to bed.

She crossed the hall to the study and tapped on the door, and, at the vague rumble from within, opened the door. 'Goodnight, Krijn,' she said quietly, and gave his bowed head a loving look.

He glanced up with impatient courtesy. 'I dare say you are tired. Goodnight, Beatrice.' She was closing the door when he added, 'There was something I had to tell you—I forget. Not now, I expect I shall think of it in the morning.'

She shut the door. If he didn't remember, she wouldn't be able to go shopping.

He did remember. When she got down to breakfast in the morning he was already at the table and beside her plate was a cheque-book and by it a bundle of notes. He got up as she went in and enquired after her night, reminded her that he would be leaving in half an hour and picked up his letters again, returning her delighted thanks with an absent-minded smile.

He drove her straight to den Haag, showed her where he would pick her up that afternoon and suggested that if he wasn't in the Hotel des Indes car park to go into the lounge and have tea. 'Don't worry if you aren't ready; I'll wait for you.'

He had got out to open her door and now stood, looming over her, looking down at her. 'That is your new suit,' he observed, 'and you were wearing that very pretty dress we bought in La Bonneterie yesterday.'

'Well,' said Trixie, 'I didn't think you noticed...'

'You must forgive me, you looked charming. You look very nice now.'

He sounded surprised and she smiled, delighted that just for a few moments he was looking at her as though he hadn't seen her before. Well, she conceded silently, he hadn't, had he? She would have to keep it up; buy clothes to catch his eye. She thought with pleasure of the wad of notes in her handbag. He had told her to spend what she wanted and she had a cheque-book with her as well. A glint of pure joy came into her eyes and he said, 'You must be thinking of something exciting, your eyes sparkle so.'

'Shopping,' she told him succinctly. 'Goodbye, Krijn.'

She had a most satisfactory day. It had been hard to turn her back on some of the more spectacular clothes; she had never had the money or the chance to wear the very latest fashions, but, much though she wished to wear the more *outré* styles, she was quite sure that as Krijn's wife she would be expected to maintain decorum and dignity. She comforted herself with the thought that she wasn't a very modern type of girl and chose instead several outfits and some more dresses, all of which, did she but know it, enhanced her quiet charm. She had more than enough money; she lunched in a quiet little café and spent the afternoon buying undies and more shoes. Krijn had told her to have everything sent to the hotel. 'They know me there,' he had said easily. 'The porter will take them in and we can collect them.'

So she arrived barely ten minutes late, with only a few small parcels, and, since there was no sign of the professor, did as she had been told and went inside to the lounge and ordered tea.

She was eyeing the dish of cream cakes, wondering if it would be greedy to have a second one, when she saw him out of the corner of her eye.

He came straight to her table, nodding to the waiter to bring him tea as he came.

He sat down opposite her. 'Hello—you've had a good day?'

'Delightful, thank you, and you?'

'Quite satisfactory. It will be pleasant to have a couple of days in Friesland. I have agreed to go to Brussels in a week's time, just for a day or so, and I must go over to Timothy's as soon as I get back from there.'

She poured his tea and handed it to him and passed him the sandwiches.

'When we get back we have been asked to dine at the university—you will meet a number of people who will scatter invitations like confetti. We have a splendid excuse in refusing them since I shall be away but I have no doubt that you will be called upon. Will you cope?'

'I expect so,' she spoke composedly, 'and I shall have Rabo to advise me.'

He nodded casually. 'We will spend Christmas in England but I should like to be back here for New Year. It is an important day for us in Holland.'

'Here or with your family?'

'Oh, the family, I should suppose. My sisters will come with their husbands and children. It is about the only time in the year when we all meet.'

He ate several sandwiches with an abstracted air, and she wondered if he had had any lunch and voiced her wonder.

'Lunch? There really wasn't time. I had coffee on the ward, though, and more coffee and a sandwich after the lecture.'

'Can you get home for lunch each day?' she wanted to know, and wished she hadn't said that at his cool,

'I've worked out a routine for myself over the years, Beatrice, and I don't feel inclined to alter it.'

She murmured gently. Given the chance she would alter it for him.

They collected her shopping presently and drove back past Leiden, through the quiet village and up to his front door to be greeted by a delighted Samson, who was immediately taken for a walk by his master, leaving Rabo and one of the maids to carry in the packages. There were a great many, thought Trixie guiltily, the guilt presently swallowed up in the delightful anticipation of what to wear that evening.

Silvery grey crêpe de Chine with a wide lace collar and a great many little buttons. Its wide skirt swirled around her in a most satisfying way and the high-heeled slippers gave her height. Delighted with her appearance she got her case from the vast cupboard and began to pack what she would need for their visit to Friesland. She would wear the new suit, she decided, take a couple of blouses and a sweater, the thick quilted jacket everyone seemed to wear in Holland, a thin wool crêpe dress and the grey one she was wearing. By the time she had filled the case it wanted only a few minutes to dinner; she went down the stairs and in to the drawing-room where Krijn sat in his chair, telephoning, and since he was speaking in Dutch she went and sat down quietly by the fire, picked up a magazine and glanced through it. He put the receiver down presently and offered her a drink and got one for himself. 'My mother,' he told her. 'She refuses to speak to you on the telephone, she wants to meet you in person first, something she is looking forward to.'

When he hadn't got his head in the clouds, the professor could be an excellent companion; dinner was a cheerful meal while he told her about Holland and the University of Leiden in a most entertaining manner, so that she almost forgave him for not noticing the grey dress. However, pleasant though the meal had been, he showed no signs of wanting to remain with her afterwards. 'We shall leave about nine o'clock tomorrow,' he told her as he put his coffee-cup down. 'I've some telephoning to do and then an hour or so of writing, so I'll say goodnight, Beatrice.'

She had had the forethought to bring a complicated piece of tapestry-work downstairs with her. She threaded a needle carefully and gave him a serene glance. 'I'm looking forward to seeing Friesland and your family,' she observed calmly. 'Goodnight, Krijn.'

She bent her head over the canvas, apparently absorbed in the work, and didn't see his slight hesitation before he went away. She took a dozen careful stitches and put it down; it made something to hide behind while she was with him but left to herself she discarded it and sat back in her chair to think.

On their way to Friesland the next morning, he told her of his family. His home was north of Leeuwarden—Veenkerk, a small village beside a lake. 'The family have lived there for a very long time. It is remote but Leeuwarden is easily reached by car, and Dokkum is only ten or twelve miles away. My father has retired and prefers to lead a quiet life.'

'Your mother likes the country?'

'Oh, yes, and the house is never empty; my sisters are all married and have children, they spend part of their school holidays there, and there is a surprisingly brisk social life, especially during the summer.'

He had chosen the route over the Afsluitdijk and they were driving around Leeuwarden by mid-morning, and then after a few miles of the motorway he turned off on to a narrow country road running between water meadows, empty of cows now. The road ran on, straight ahead, with nothing to disturb it, although on either side there were farms crouching in front of their vast barns. Presently she saw trees ahead of her and the outline of a jelly-mould church.

'Veenkerk,' said the professor. 'We're rather out on the other side of the village.'

The village was small with two outsize churches, a shop or two and a small market square. The professor drove through it along a narrow street with a high wall on one side and then turned into a narrow lane between trees. Trixie could see the house at its end . . .

'It's a castle!' she exclaimed.

'No, it's a Middle Ages red-brick house called a *stins*; we have no castles as such and not many of the *stinsen* remain.'

'Oh, does it have a name?'

'Schaakslot. Of course not much of the original *stins* exists; my ancestors built over and around them and they were called *staten* so in fact the place is Schaak-State.'

'It's a bit confusing.'

He had nothing to say to this but drew up before the front door, a stoutly built affair set in the centre of the house; there were windows on either side, a circular tower at one corner and a larger square one at the other. A row of windows, much smaller than those on the ground floor, was overhung by a sloping roof in which were a number of dormer windows, and a wide bridge over a moat led to the front door.

The professor got out, came round to open her door, let Samson out from the back of the car and took her arm, crossed the bridge and reached the door as it was opened.

An old man stood there to greet them, white-haired and with a slight stoop and very neatly dressed. The professor shook his hand, exchanged a few words and said, 'Beatrice, this is Wiber; he has been with the family since I was born.'

She shook hands and encountered a pair of faded blue eyes studying her searchingly. *'Welkom, mevrouw,'* he said, and he took her hand in a surprisingly firm grip, gave it back to her gently and led the way into a large panelled hall, which had a lofty ceiling of elaborate plasterwork, and, facing the door, a massive staircase with a half-landing and two wings leading to the gallery above. On either side of the staircase was a door; one of green baize led, she imagined, to the kitchen; the other had a wide glass panel through which she glimpsed a garden. They were halfway across the hall when a pair of arched doors were thrown open and two people came to meet them. There was no doubt that the elderly gentleman was Krijn's father—they shared the same good looks—but it was his companion who surprised her, a small stout lady, dressed in the manner in which elderly stout ladies should be dressed, her hair in an uncompromising bun, anchored to the top of her head and none the less very elegant. She trotted ahead of her husband, flung her arms around her son's neck and embraced him before turning to Trixie. 'And this is our new daughter. Welcome, Beatrice, my dear.' She embraced Trixie too, her blue eyes twinkling from a round face, so charming that it could have been mistaken for prettiness. Her husband, greeting Krijn, was plucked on the coat sleeve. 'Wildrik, here is Beatrice at last. Is she not exactly right for Krijn? Have I not always said that when at last he marries it would be worth the waiting?'

Her husband took Trixie's hand and bent to kiss her cheek. 'Welcome, Beatrice. I can but add my delight at meeting you. Come into the drawing-room and meet the family.'

He took her arm and ushered her into a long wide room which to her bemused eyes appeared full of people. There were, in fact, Krijn's sisters there with seven children and one man, who turned round to look at her as they went in. Trixie, introduced to them all in turn, found herself standing in front of him while Krijn said easily, 'Oh, this is Andre ter Vange, one of our very numerous cousins. Andre, this is my wife, Beatrice; be a good chap and take her round once more so that she gets the names right—there are so many of us!'

He smiled down at Trixie. 'Andre knows all there is to know about us; he'll fill in all the gaps. I'll be back...'

Andre smiled at her charmingly, and he had charm; he was good-looking too with a friendly smile. He said, 'Delighted—always glad to welcome another cousin into the family. I'll take care of your Beatrice, Krijn.'

Trixie stood between them, wishing that she could have stayed with Krijn but fair enough to realise that he might want to spend a little time with his parents. Krijn went away presently and Andre led her to a windowseat. 'Time enough to get to know everyone,' he said easily. 'Let's start with us...'

When she didn't say anything he said, 'I'm about the only man in the family who isn't something to do with medicine. I'm an architect. I've worked in England and

America, I live in den Haag and I travel a good deal. I'm thirty years old and I'm not married.' He grinned at her. 'Now you.'

He was friendly and amusing and he was trying to put her at her ease, something which Krijn should have done, she reflected uneasily. She said in her matter-of-fact way, 'I'm not anything really—I was training to be a nurse...before that I lived with an aunt and uncle in London—my parents died...'

'And along comes Krijn and sweeps you off your feet. Well, well, how romantic; there must be a side to him that I haven't encountered.'

She frowned. 'He's the kindest and nicest man I have ever met and I dare say you don't meet him enough to know much about him.'

He was quick to see the flash of anger in her eyes. 'Sorry—Krijn is a marvellous man and brilliantly clever. He has a reputation all over Europe—he's been to America too. It's marvellous that he's decided to marry at last.'

He spoke pleasantly, but Trixie had the feeling that he didn't really mean what he was saying. It was a relief when Soeske, the eldest sister, joined them. She took Trixie's arm. 'You've had Beatrice long enough,' she declared. 'Mama wants to talk to her.' She swept Trixie away to where her mother was talking to Krijn.

'Here she is,' said Soeske. 'Krijn, come and talk to the children and let Mama get to know Beatrice.'

'You must feel a little bewildered, my dear—so many of us and all of us talking at once. We see Krijn seldom and when we do we all try to be here together to exchange news.' Mevrouw van der Brink-Schaaksma took Trixie's hand and added, 'Come and sit down and tell me all about yourself. Krijn is shockingly bad at writing letters and how can anyone describe the girl he's going to marry over the telephone? We have all been dying of curiosity.'

Trixie said in her sensible way, 'Well, I hope I'll do. I've been curious about you too—and a bit scared.'

'Bless you, child, no need of that,' said her companion comfortably. 'You have no idea how pleased we all are that Krijn has at last decided to take a wife.'

'That's what Andre said...'

'Andre is very clever at saying the right thing; he can put anyone at their ease within minutes. He's a most successful architect.' Mevrouw van der Brink-Schaaksma spoke pleasantly so that Trixie, who had had the feeling that her hostess didn't like the young man, decided that she was mistaken. She sat there for some time, answering her companion's gentle questions while she wondered if Krijn had told his parents that he had married for convenience and not for love. She thought it unlikely.

Presently Krijn joined them. 'May I take Beatrice away, Mama,' he wanted to know, 'while I help her sort out the children?'

'Of course, dear, and then perhaps Beatrice would like to go up to your room—you're in the round tower—so thoughtless of us not to have thought of that first, but we were so anxious to see you both.'

So half an hour later, her head full of childish faces and unpronounceable names, Trixie was taken upstairs by Reka—another sister—and led along a corridor leading from the gallery to a small door with an old-fashioned latch. It opened on to a lobby which in turn led to a circular room with a wide bay window, a massive canopied bed and much mahogany furniture decorated with marquetry. The pair of them went to look out of the windows and Reka said, 'Isn't it a lovely view? So peaceful. The park ends at that row of trees there, there's a canal round the back of the house but quite a lot of ground on either side. Do you like it?'

'I think it's simply marvellous...'

'Do you like us? Are we anything like you expected?'

'I think you're all marvellous, too. I'm so happy to have a family.'

'Krijn is a darling, but of course you know that, don't you?'

'Yes, I do.' They smiled at each other, and Reka said, 'I'll leave you for a few minutes. We're at the other end of the corridor—I'll be back.'

She went away and Trixie went round poking her nose round doors. The first one was a clothing cupboard, the second a bathroom of superlative elegance, the third led to another bathroom, and, beyond that, a smaller bedroom with the bed made up, and Trixie, who had been a little worried but hadn't liked to mention it, heaved a small sigh of relief.

She did her face and tidied her hair and went back to the window, just in time to see Krijn strolling down one of the paths below, his arm around his mother's shoulder while Samson and two small dogs pranced around them.

For a moment she squeezed her eyes shut on sudden tears, then turned to smile at Reka as she tapped on the door and came in. 'Ready?' She came to stand by Trixie. 'Mama will be doing her best to find out all about you— not you, I mean how you met and if he fell in love at once or whether he just found that he wanted to marry you. Did he? Did he fall in love at once or after you'd got to know each other?'

Trixie spoke slowly. 'I think he—he just wanted to marry me.' Which was, after all, the truth.

'You don't mind me asking? I won't tell anyone...'

'Of course I don't mind.'

They went back downstairs and presently went into lunch, sitting round a very large circular table, with the older children sandwiched between their elders and the littlest ones in high chairs. Trixie, with Krijn beside her and her father-in-law at the head of the table on her other side, looked around her. The room was large and the table could accommodate twenty persons without difficulty. The side-table was of carved oak and laden with massive silver and a Friese clock hung on the wall above it. The windows here were long and narrow with heavy crimson curtains and elaborate pelmets. It could have been a set piece in some museum but it wasn't; it was lived in, used daily by people who took its magnificence for granted but cherished it too.

Lunch was simple, beautifully served and eaten at leisure. 'There will be the rest of the family this evening,' said her father-in-law. 'The girls' husbands. Everyone will stay the night, of course.'

He was very like Krijn; Trixie wondered if he was absent-minded. Between father and son she was kept entertained throughout the meal and since the table was round there was a good deal of over-the-table talk. She saw Andre looking at her and smiled at him; he had been friendly and kind, putting her at her ease, but she wasn't sure if she liked him. However, he was Krijn's cousin and she was prepared to like anyone or anything to do with him...

They showed her the park that afternoon, bundled in old coats and jackets from the boot-room beside the stout back door. She was passed from one member of the family to the other while the older children milled around and the dogs raced ahead, and for a little while she found herself walking with Andre, who laid himself out to be charming and amusing, but she was glad when she found herself back again beside Krijn's vast reassuring person. He took her arm and told her about the house and the family, and although he made no attempt to be either amusing or charming she listened to his quiet voice with delight and deep content. Looking up into his calm face she promised herself that she would do everything in her power to make him happy, and, if that meant hours spent all alone while he worked on his book or travelled all over the place for consultations or lectures, then she would do it gladly. Loving someone, she reflected soberly, wasn't the same thing as falling in love; she had done both and perhaps she was fortunate to have done so, even though it would bring heartache.

That evening Gabe, Edwer, Alco and Bruno arrived in time for dinner, solid young men who assured her in turn that they were delighted that Krijn had found himself a wife at last and one so obviously just right for him. 'The girls have been matchmaking for him for years,' Gabe told her, 'but he never took any notice. We were beginning to think that he was going to remain a bachelor, so you can imagine how pleased we all were when he told us he was going to marry.' He twinkled nicely at her. 'And such a nice girl too. Will you be here for Christmas?'

'I don't think so. Krijn has to go back to Timothy's before then . . .'

'You'll be here for Oud en Nieuw—he never misses that. New Year is an important date in our calendar.'

'Then I'm sure we'll be here.'

She went upstairs to change for dinner with Krijn, and he paused at her door to ask her if she had everything she needed. 'I'll knock in about half an hour,' he told her, and walked on down to his dressing-room door.

They went downstairs together presently and she was glad that she had packed the grey dress; she knew that it suited her and despite its simplicity it had the hallmark of expensive elegance. At the foot of the stairs Krijn paused to look at her. 'That's a pretty dress—I haven't seen it before...'

Dinner—smoked salmon, roast pheasant with a great many garnishes and red cabbage, profiteroles, oozing cream and dripping chocolate sauce with a lemon sorbet after the pheasant and cheese and biscuits to round off the meal—was a leisurely affair with everyone talking at once and a good deal of laughter, and presently they all went back to the drawing-room for coffee and more talk. It was late when Mevrouw van der Brink-Schaaksma said that she was going to bed and invited any one wishing to do so to accompany her. The women went willingly, leaving the men to their talk, and Trixie, making her round of goodnights, was glad that it was Krijn who went to the door to open it as she, the last, went past him. He put a hand on her shoulder, dropped a kiss on her cheek and bent to wish her goodnight so quietly that no one else could have heard. A good thing too, she thought, aware that they were being watched by the remaining men.

It had been an exciting day; she slept soundly and since, after breakfast, it began to rain for a time as there was a lowering sky, she was taken on a tour of the house. Luisje, the youngest of Krijn's sisters, went with her and so did his mother, and since they paused frequently to examine a piece of furniture or study a painting it was lunchtime before they had finished.

In the afternoon there was more talk round the fire, then everyone started to leave for home. Krijn and Beatrice were the last to go and she, getting into the car and turning to wave at his father and mother standing on the steps of the house, felt regret that their stay had been so brief. She had dreaded it and that had been silly of her; it had been delightful and Krijn's family had been more than kind. She had had enough invitations to last her for months and Andre had asked if he might call. 'I am nearer than anyone else,' he had told her, 'and I'd love to drop in for coffee now and again.'

She had agreed because it was the obvious thing to do. She told Krijn that as they drove back to Leiden and he had answered her briefly. 'Oh, good. Andre is an amusing companion and he seems to have more time on his hands than the rest of us.' He hadn't said any more and she guessed that he was already thinking of tomorrow's work that lay ahead of him.

It was nearly evening when they reached the house, and Rabo welcomed them with the offer of coffee. They went into the drawing-room together and Krijn sat down to look through his letters. There had been messages from the hospital too, and as Trixie poured their first cups the telephone rang.

It was a lengthy conversation and she understood nothing of it beyond his brief *'ja'* or *'neen'*. He put the phone down at length. 'I'm afraid I must go into Leiden. Don't wait dinner for me, Beatrice. Wolke will get me something later if I need it.'

'Is it something very urgent?'

He was halfway to the door. 'Yes. I'll see you at breakfast.'

CHAPTER SIX

IT WAS on the evening after their return from Schaakslot that Krijn told Trixie that they would be going to dinner at the university in Leiden on the following day.

'Gracious, what short notice, and what do I wear?'

'Did I not tell you? It might have slipped my mind. Wear anything pretty.'

She wished to be fair. 'You mentioned that we would be going when we got back but you didn't say when. Perhaps I misunderstood you...'

She went to bed that evening worrying about the right clothes: long or short, dressed up or casual? She woke several times during the night and went down to her breakfast looking wan with the lack of sleep.

'You do not feel well?' asked Krijn. 'You are pale—you have not slept?'

She stared down at her plate. 'It's really very silly. I don't know what to wear to this dinner party—I don't want to make you feel ashamed of me...'

He said gravely, 'I don't think that would be possible, Beatrice. I'm sure that you will look very nice whatever you decide to wear.'

A remark which was of no help at all although she agreed quickly. After all, he had other things to think about and certainly wouldn't want to be bothered with her clothes.

The professor wasn't exactly bothered, but Beatrice was a nice girl and he didn't like to see her looking anything but cheerful. They were good friends, he reminded himself, and as such he felt called upon to do something about it. At the hospital he telephoned Mevrouw van Vliet, who was giving the dinner party.

Trixie was arranging chrysanthemums in a Delft vase when the phone rang, and Mevrouw van Vliet wished her good morning in the precise, heavily accented English she spoke. 'We have not met but I hear good things of you, and we look forward to meeting this evening. There will be many people to wish you well. It is an occasion, you understand? The men will wear the smok-ing——'

'The what?' asked Trixie, getting a word in edgeways.

'You say the dinner-jacket? The ladies the long skirt, for we shall dance after dinner.'

'It sounds delightful; I'm looking forward to meeting Krijn's friends and colleagues.'

'We see you at eight o'clock. May I call you Beatrice? That is your name, Krijn tells us.'

'Yes, of course, Mevrouw van Vliet; we look forward to the evening.'

She put down the receiver and skipped upstairs to spend the next half-hour deciding what to wear. Mevrouw van Vliet had sounded a bit intimidating; presumably she was the senior lady at the university—if there was such a thing. She would play safe and wear something suitable for a professor's wife. She laid her new evening gowns on the bed. On the other hand she didn't want to look a frump, although that would be hard even in the plainest of the dresses.

She chose a rose-patterned chiffon with a wide floating skirt, a modest neckline and elbow-length sleeves. It was a pretty dress and there was nothing about it to allow of criticism.

Krijn wouldn't be home for lunch. She ate hers with Percy for company and then got into the sensible rain-proof jacket she had bought in den Haag, got out her stout shoes, and walked down to the village, where she bought postcards and stamps at the village shop, responded suitably to those she met—and there seemed to be a great many people about. She wasn't to know that the news had spread like wildfire that the professor's wife was buying postcards so that any number of house-wives came into the shop to buy tea and sugar they didn't need just to get a close look at her.

She was, after all, a foreigner.

Krijn wasn't home by half-past six. Determined not to get uptight, Trixie went upstairs to dress. It was after seven o'clock when she went downstairs again. She was at the foot of the staircase as he let himself in and he stood for a moment, looking at her.

'Very nice, Beatrice.' He sounded like a good-natured brother anxious to say the right thing, she thought peevishly.

However, her 'Hello, Krijn, have you had a busy day? Would you like something to eat before you dress?' was said in exactly the right kind of voice, solicitous without sounding anxious.

'Nothing, thanks. I'd better change.' He glanced at his watch as he walked to his study. 'We don't need to leave until eight o'clock—it's only ten minutes in the car.'

Samson and Percy kept her company by the fire in the small sitting-room she used when Krijn wasn't home and she employed the time in picking out words from the advertisements in the *Algemeen Dagblad*. She was beginning to understand simple sentences by now and she had bought a dictionary and a grammar, although she was unable to make head nor tail of the latter. She put it down thankfully as the professor came into the room and got up with alacrity to wrap herself in the velvet coat he had picked up from a chair.

He said, laughing, 'You are all eagerness, Beatrice. You will find everyone very friendly, and don't worry about your lack of Dutch—everyone there will speak English.'

She said coldly, feeling hurt, 'I shall ask advice as to the best teacher so that I can feel more at home...' She saw his faint frown and added, 'I mean—at home with the language.'

'Remind me of that; I believe I know just the person. Shall we go?'

It was a short drive into Leiden and across the Rapenburg Canal to the university and they had little to say. Trixie, sitting a little sideways so that she could see Krijn's profile and watch his large, well-kept hands on the wheel, was content to stay silent save for the odd murmur; for her part she could have spent the rest of the evening sitting there beside him. Being in love was very upsetting, she reflected as Krijn drew up before the university and got out to open her door before the doorman had the chance. He said something to him and the man got into the car and drove it away as they went inside.

In the vast entrance hall he gave her a friendly shove. 'Off you go and leave your coat. I'll be here.'

She was led away, to return presently, scared that he might have forgotten about her and entered into some deep discussion with one of the other learned gentlemen present, but he was there, just exactly where he had said that he would be, and they went together to be greeted by the various members of the university. In no time at all she had forgotten the names of the people to whom she was introduced, but Mevrouw van Vliet, who had sounded rather awe-inspiring on the telephone, was kindness itself. True, she was a formidable figure, draped in plum-coloured velvet and with a severe hairstyle, but her small blue eyes twinkled nicely as she took Trixie away from Krijn and led her round the other ladies already there, and then left her with her husband, who was to take her in to dinner. 'For you are the guests of honour,' she explained kindly. 'We at the medical school are so delighted that Krijn has married. He has had his nose buried in his books and papers for far too long.'

Dinner was long and formal and Krijn was at the other end of the long table, sitting next to his hostess. Trixie thought that her host was very like old Colonel Vosper and she gave him her full attention, so that he told his wife later that evening that Krijn had done very well for himself.

'She is right for him, perhaps a little old-fashioned but *deftig*,' and his wife nodded in agreement. Beatrice would do very well; she had dignity, decorum and obviously came from a respectable background and that, after all, was the essence of *deftigheid*.

An opinion the rest of the company shared, and lost no time in telling Krijn what a very fortunate man he was to have such a delightful wife. He accepted their congratulations gravely and when everyone had gone into the adjoining room, cleared for dancing, he took her arm and said quietly, 'I believe that we are to start the ball rolling...'

They circled the room, and she trembled a little in his arms.

'Are you cold? No—nervous. No need, you are a great success, you know.'

He looked down at her and smiled and she said, 'Oh, good,' and everyone clapped and started dancing as well.

She danced for the rest of the evening, and was handed from one scholarly gentleman to another. None of them was young; there were several about the same age as Krijn but for the most part they were dignified and with a proper sense of their worth, but to a man they were kind and she couldn't help but see they admired her. Their wives were kind too; mindful of Krijn's advice, she accepted invitations to coffee and tea but was politely vague about evening engagements. 'Krijn has to go to Brussels,' she told the various ladies. 'I'm not at all sure how long he'll be away and when he returns he will have a backlog of work...' She explained 'backlog' carefully and received their sympathetic glances.

'But naturally, we do understand,' they chorused. 'And besides, you have so little chance of being alone together.'

On their way home she told him what she had said.

'Splendid,' he observed. 'Go to all the tea parties you want. When I am home we shall be left to ourselves for a few weeks at least. I hope to get another chapter written before we go back to England.'

Trixie sought for a suitable answer to this and decided that there wasn't one. She loved him—she was in love with him too—but surely he was the most selfish man on earth—or the most single-minded one. Did he never think of anything but his work? She asked rather tartly, 'And in England?'

'I have no doubt that you will contrive to avoid too many social occasions. We shall, of course, be expected to give a dinner party, or perhaps, since it will be Christmas, we might have people in for drinks?'

'I'll do my best,' said Trixie. 'I liked your friends.'

'They liked you too. I can safely leave the social life to you, Beatrice.'

They were home now, standing in the hall in the silent house. 'I'll do my best,' she said again. 'Krijn, was there one particular girl or were there several girls who—who got between you and your work?'

He said without conceit, 'Not one in particular, but yes, there were several. You see, they all thought that I would be so much better off married. You know the argument: someone to come home to, children, visits to the theatre, dinner out, entertaining...'

'Of course they all came between you and your book.' She spoke in her usual calm manner, but he gave her a keen look.

'Yes. You find that difficult to understand?'

'No, at least not unless you were in love with any of them.'

He paused to think. 'In love—perhaps a little, but that is hardly the same as loving a woman to the exclusion of all else and that I imagine is the only valid reason for marrying.'

'But you married me...'

'An entirely different matter.' He had picked up a handful of messages left on the wall table and was reading them. 'Goodnight, Beatrice. I don't expect I shall see you at breakfast but I should be home soon after midday tomorrow.'

She asked in a voice devoid of expression, 'You will have lunch here?'

He glanced up. 'That rather depends—don't wait for me, I may get a sandwich at the hospital.'

He smiled suddenly with such charm that she blinked at him and said meekly, 'Goodnight, Krijn.'

He watched her cross the hall and start up the staircase. He reached it at the same time as she did. 'Beatrice, you are happy here? Is there anything you want? You are not lonely or homesick?'

She climbed two or three treads so that she was on a level with him. 'I am very happy, thank you, Krijn, and certainly not lonely or homesick.' It seemed prudent not to tell him that what she wanted more than anything else on earth was him. She sensed that he wasn't satisfied with her answer, though.

'I should very much like to have Dutch lessons,' she told him, 'and I wonder if there is something I could do? I mean, a day nursery or visiting old people or...' She faltered for a moment. 'You see, I'm not used to doing nothing.' Her voice died away; she sounded like a priggish do-gooder.

His hand came down on hers in a firm clasp. 'Of course you shall have Dutch lessons—I'll arrange them for you tomorrow. There is a crèche in the village—quite a few of the younger women go to Leiden to work and I think the women who run it would be glad of help. Leave it to me.'

He bent and kissed her cheek. 'Sleep well.'

It was a surprise to her when he came home the next afternoon accompanied by a severe-looking lady of middle years and introduced her as Juffrouw van der Bos who had agreed to give her lessons each morning at a time convenient to Trixie and suggested that directly after breakfast might be a good time before Trixie needed to take up her household duties.

Trixie, whose household duties were negligible, agreed at once. Juffrouw van der Bos, after drinking coffee with them, was driven away by Rabo in the Jaguar which was housed with the Bentley and the small Fiat Rabo used for running errands.

'Thank you,' said Trixie, 'I'm awfully grateful.'

Krijn was on his way to the door, Samson at his heels. 'Juffrouw van der Bos looks fierce, but she's a splendid teacher. I have to make a phone call, but perhaps you might like to walk down to the village with me presently and have a look at the crèche.'

'Oh, Krijn, yes please.'

It had turned very cold; she got into her quilted jacket, dragged a cap over her neat hair and found a pair of old woolly gloves. She was waiting for him when he came out of his study and presently they set out with Samson pacing beside them.

There was a short cut through the grounds of the house which brought them out very close to the village square, so that their walk was a short one during which the professor kept up a steady flow of small talk. No one listening to us, thought Trixie, would believe that we were man and wife. Yet, when they reached the poky village hall where the crèche was housed, she had to admit that he gave a very good impression of a thoughtful husband. She was introduced to the two middle-aged women who ran it, and, without her doing much about it, she found herself committed to three mornings a week from nine o'clock in the morning until noon. 'And you don't need to worry about the language problems; the children are babies or toddlers and I imagine that you will be chiefly concerned with feeding, or changing nappies and so forth.'

Krijn listened to what the elder of the two women had to say. 'You're quite sure that you want to do it?' he asked Trixie. 'And it is strictly on the understanding that if other commitments should arise they will take precedence.'

'Yes, I understand, and I'd like very much to help if they will have me.'

The women smilingly nodded, not understanding what she was saying but sensing that she wanted to help them. She shook their hands once more and walked back with Krijn. 'Who runs the crèche?' she asked. 'I mean there's the rent and things like kettles and basins and babies' bottles and so on...'

'I do. I regret that I seldom go there; I must rely on you to let me know if anything is needed.'

'Supposing the babies are ill? Do they have to go to Leiden?'

'If it's something minor I deal with it, otherwise I send them to Leiden.' He added, 'I'm not a paediatrician.'

'No. I know,' she sounded a little tart, 'though I suppose you know about a great deal besides glands?'

'Well, yes, but one tends to channel one's interest...'

You can say that again, reflected Trixie sourly.

On the following day he drove off to Brussels but not before asking her if there was anything she needed advice on, and warning her once again of the invitations they might expect to receive. 'I'm sure,' he told her smoothly, 'that you will be able to deal with them.'

'When will you be back?'

'I can't be certain. When I go to Brussels I usually call upon friends and perhaps stay overnight. I will phone you.'

She saw him off from the steps outside the door with Samson beside her. To the casual eye, she appeared to be a happy wife speeding her husband on his way, but as she waved to the fast-disappearing car she wondered who the friends were...

She went to the crèche that morning and despite the small difficulties of communication she enjoyed herself. It was lovely to have something else to do and the crèche was over-full. Quite small babies who needed feeding and changing, toddlers whose mothers left home early each morning and didn't get back until late afternoon; it was surprising that in so small a village so many of the younger women went out to work. She went home to lunch feeling quite cheerful to find the post had come, and, sure enough, most of it was invitations to dinner, evening drinks and a birthday party for Professor someone-or-other. There were invitations for her too: coffee at various houses and requests for her to join various charitable societies. If she joined them all she wouldn't have a moment to spare...

She spent the afternoon sorting them out and then set about answering them. The dinner parties she started off with, making the quite true excuse that Krijn hadn't been certain as to which day he would return and could she let their hostess know later? The coffee-mornings she accepted; if she didn't her new acquaintances might wonder why, and they might even dislike her for it. She additionally agreed to join several of the charity committees too because it was expected of her. It was a relief when Krijn telephoned that evening; she hadn't expected it and she beamed at the receiver as she lifted it, so that Rabo, who had taken the call, went back to the kitchen to tell Wolke that *mevrouw* had shown all the proper sentiments at getting a call from the professor.

'Quite right too,' said Wolke. 'They've only been married for such a short time; such a pity she couldn't go with him.'

Rabo muttered the Dutch equivalent to "absence makes the heart grow fonder", and added that she would be going back to England with the professor very shortly. 'And a nicer young lady I've yet to meet.'

'You're all right?' Krijn's voice sent a little thrill through her person. 'How was the crèche?'

'Marvellous, I loved every minute of it. There were a lot of letters...' She told him about them. 'The only one I've not answered is the birthday party.'

'Accept it. He's an old professor of anatomy—must be nudging eighty. His wife gives him a splendid party each year.'

'It's in a week's time. Will you be back?'

'Yes.'

He didn't add to that so she asked, 'Have you had a busy day?'

'Yes. I'm phoning from a friend's house in Brussels. I'm dining there.'

She curbed her tongue from uttering, Who with? and said lamely, 'How nice.' When he remained silent she observed that Samson was missing him. In the silence which followed she heard a woman's voice calling him.

'Well, I mustn't keep you from your friends.' She was rather pleased with the casual way in which she said that. 'Goodbye, Krijn.'

'Goodnight, Beatrice.' He sounded as though he was laughing.

She didn't know if he would ring on the following day, although she hoped that he would. He didn't, however, and on the day after that she went to the crèche again.

It was a wet, cold morning but after the warmth and noise in the crèche she was glad to walk back through the rain, thinking about Krijn, wondering what he was doing and when he would be back home. Her heart leapt when she saw the car before the house, only to plummet into the foot of her shoes when she saw that it wasn't the Bentley. She hurried her steps, intent on getting into the house. It might be someone with a message from Krijn or someone who had seen him in Brussels. Heedless of the rain-wet face and her untidy head, she cast off her jacket and headscarf as she went through a side door and gained the hall. Rabo came to meet her.

'A visitor, *mevrouw*. One of the professor's cousins, Mijnheer Andre ter Vange.'

'Oh, yes. We met at Veenkerk. Is he in the drawing-room, Rabo?'

'Yes, *mevrouw*. Will he be staying for lunch?'

'Well, I dare say. I'll ask him and let you know.'

She paused to smooth her hair and went into the drawing-room, to find Andre lounging in a chair by the fire while Samson sat by Krijn's chair opposite, watching him.

He got up when he saw Trixie and so did the dog. She patted Samson's great head and offered a hand to Andre.

'How nice to see you, but I'm afraid Krijn isn't here— he's in Brussels...'

'Yes, I know. I thought you might be feeling lonely. Am I invited to lunch?'

'Of course...'

'We'll go for a drive this afternoon and perhaps you'll invite me back for tea—even dinner? We must get to know each other.'

'How kind of you, but I can't do that. The dominee's wife is coming here at two o'clock to talk about St Nikolaas—that's the day after tomorrow. I'm going to help with the children in the village and I said I'd give a hand wrapping up presents.'

'Good lord, Beatrice, do you have to act the matron? These people can manage quite well by themselves. I counted on us spending the rest of the day together.'

'Well, I'm sorry but I said I would help...'

His smile held a faint sneer. 'Oh, well, another time.' He got up. 'I'll be going.'

'I thought you were staying for lunch?'

'I've just remembered I've a client coming at one o'clock.' She walked with him to the door and he took her hand. 'We really shall have to get to know each other; I shall come again. When is Krijn coming back?'

She didn't know what prompted her to say, 'Oh, probably today or early tomorrow.'

'Just my luck. He'll want you all to himself, won't he?'

'Oh, yes,' she said steadily. It had been kind of him to come, she reflected, waving goodbye from the steps, but she still wasn't sure if she liked him.

The dominee's wife was a bit overpowering; her English was good, which made her feel superior in the first place, and she had lived in the village for so long that she took it for granted that what she said was law there.

Trixie, over coffee and little sugary biscuits, refused to be browbeaten by that lady's somewhat hectoring ways and presently accompanied her to the village where, in the dominee's house, there were oranges and sweets and small presents waiting to be wrapped in bright paper.

'Do people give you all these?' asked Trixie, and blushed when the dominee's wife told her severely that every household was expected to subscribe a small amount.

'As it is, we are always short of money, *mevrouw*.'

'Oh, then please allow me to help. I'm sure if the professor were here——'

'Well, he is,' said Krijn's voice just behind her. When she turned in surprised delight, he said, 'Forgive me, Mevrouw Kraan; the door was open.'

He bent and kissed Trixie's cheek, observing, 'I have returned rather earlier than I anticipated,' and then shook hands with Mevrouw Kraan. 'I'm glad to see that my wife is taking part in the preparations for St Nikolaas, but I must beg you to allow her to come home. I am, as I said, earlier than I expected.'

In the car, driving the short distance to the house, he observed, 'Mevrouw Kraan is rather a dragon...'

'Yes, I know. You didn't phone.'

He sounded concerned. 'It quite slipped my mind. Have I spoilt your afternoon?'

She turned a happy face to his. 'Oh, no. I'm so glad you're back.'

They went indoors and when she would have gone upstairs to take off her outdoor things he said impatiently, 'Let them stay there for the moment. We'll have coffee in the drawing-room, shall we?'

Sitting by the fire with a delighted Samson between their chairs, he said, 'You have not been lonely?'

What would he say if she told him that she counted every minute until he returned? 'Not a bit. I have had a Dutch lesson and Samson and I went for walks and there was the crèche.' She paused to pour their coffee.

'When I got back from the crèche this morning, Andre was here. He said he'd come for lunch and wanted to take me out for a drive afterwards, but of course I couldn't because I'd already promised Mevrouw Kraan that I'd help here. I did ask him to stay for lunch only then he remembered that he had a client at one o'clock, so he went away again. I told him that you were in Brussels and...' She paused then.

The professor asked, 'And what, Beatrice?'

'I do hope you don't mind; I said you were coming back today...'

He asked placidly, 'You had a reason?'

'Well, I do hope you won't be annoyed, only he said he would come back to take me out for a day.' She gave him a direct look. 'I know he's your cousin, but he seemed to think that I needed company.' She added hastily, 'He's very kind and friendly.'

The professor ignored that. 'And do you need company, Beatrice?'

'Me? Oh, no. I am going to have coffee with Mevrouw van Vliet to meet some of the ladies who were at the dinner.'

Percy had come to join them and had climbed on to her lap, and she bent to stroke him. 'That's unless you want me to do anything else...'

'My dear Beatrice, I have no intention of interfering in your plans, but I must remind you that we shall be returning to England in five days' time.' He put down his cup. 'There are several cases waiting for me at Timothy's, and Mrs Grey has made a number of appointments. We will spend Christmas there, and perhaps you will let your aunt know—if you remember she suggested that we might like to dine with them.'

'Very well, I'll do that,' Trixie agreed quietly, not wanting to do anything of the sort. 'Will you be at home all day tomorrow?'

'I'm afraid not, though I'll probably be back in the late afternoon.'

'Several people phoned to know when you would be back, but I said I wasn't sure. The only invitation I accepted for us both is that birthday party in three days' time.'

'Ah, yes. What are you doing tomorrow?'

'Well, there's no crèche but I said I'd help get the place ready for St Nikolaas and then the afternoon will be taken up with several people coming to tea. They'll be gone by the time that you get home.'

He got to his feet and she saw then that he was tired. 'I'll do some writing until dinner,' he observed. 'Will you tell Rabo not to disturb me? He'll take any phone calls. If it's anything urgent he will let me know.'

He went away with Samson at his heels and presently Trixie went upstairs, where, for no reason at all, she curled up on her bed and had a good cry.

Not for long, however; it would never do for Krijn to notice her red eyes and pink nose. She must remember that she was a sensible girl who knew what was expected of her; ready to be good company if the occasion arose and fend off tiresome intruders into Krijn's own serious world and accept gracefully his comings and goings. A kind of devoted personal assistant, she told her reflection as she inspected her face for signs of tears.

She went back to the drawing-room then and applied herself to her tapestry until Rabo brought in the tea-tray. 'And don't on any account disturb the professor, will you, Rabo?' she begged.

Later, when she had come downstairs again after changing into a dress for the evening, she found Krijn sitting in his chair with the faithful Samson beside him. He got up as she went in. 'What would you like to drink?' and when he had poured it he sat down again, a glass of Jenever at his elbow.

'I hope Rabo didn't have to disturb you,' said Trixie. 'Dinner won't be for another half-hour.'

She didn't get an answer to that. The professor regarded her thoughtfully, aware that he had missed her while he had been away; it was something that he would have to think about once he had completed the chapter which needed his meticulous attention at the moment.

'Will you be sorry to leave here?' he asked idly.

'Oh, yes. But we shall be coming back later...'

'Yes, in time for New Year—we shall spend that with the family. Could you cope if they come here and stay overnight?'

She nodded her mousy head. 'Rabo and Wolke will advise me, won't they? Everyone will come on Old Year's Day, I expect? For lunch?'

'Tea, and a rather special dinner, and friends join us afterwards. Everyone goes again after lunch on New Year's Day.'

'Will we be back in time for us to plan meals and see to the rooms and all that?'

'We shall be back on December the twenty-ninth. You will have rather more than a full day, but Wolke will see to the rooms while we are in London, and perhaps you could discuss the food before we go.'

'Yes, I'll do that.' She would have liked more time to make plans, but there was no point in saying so; she had several days before they were to leave for England and Wolke was a tower of strength.

They dined, well-pleased with each other's company, their talk the casual conversation of friends although it never touched upon themselves. Later, the professor went back to his writing, but before he picked up his pen he sat back in his chair to reflect upon the successful outcome of his marriage. Already Beatrice was coping with the social life he wanted, for the most part, to avoid; she was a quiet girl and a splendid listener and he found her company restful. She had slipped neatly into the niche he had envisaged for her and she seemed perfectly content with her life. He smiled a little, remembering her tumble on the ward at Timothy's; he had barely noticed her then and yet he hadn't forgotten her either. There was a great deal to be said for a marriage such as theirs, unencumbered by romance. That was something he had avoided since his youthful affair with a girl who had sworn to wait for him until he had qualified as a doctor and had thrown him over for an Argentinian cattle baron. He had immersed himself in his profession after that and now, after all those years, the girl quite forgotten, habit had taken over and his work was paramount.

He gladly took up his pen and began a fresh paragraph appertaining to the ductless glands.

CHAPTER SEVEN

KRIJN was already at breakfast when Trixie went into the dining-room the next morning and before she was halfway through her toast he got up to go. 'I did tell you that I would be home later this afternoon?' he asked her, and, when she assured him that he had, 'If the ladies are still here I shall creep in through a side-door,' and when she nodded he said, 'What a splendid stand-in you are. Hopefully those who have felt impelled to entertain me, under the impression that a bachelor needs female company at all times, will transfer their good intentions to you, Beatrice. I believe that married women love young brides.'

Bridegrooms love young brides too, thought Trixie, but kept the thought to herself.

She had her Dutch lesson directly after breakfast, ploughing her eager way through verbs and phrases with such enthusiasm that her stern teacher felt compelled to praise her, and, at the same time, give her a great deal of studying to do before the next lesson. 'A great pity that you will be in England for several weeks,' she commented. 'It is to be hoped that you will continue your studies there. We will discuss that when I come again.'

It was time to nip down to the village and finish wrapping the small presents ready for St Nikolaas to hand round on the following day. Mevrouw Kraan was disposed to be friendly and Trixie, wrapping marzipan figures in bright paper, enjoyed herself. 'You will, of course, come to church on Sunday,' said Mevrouw Kraan.

'If the professor is free I shall come with him,' Trixie told her, and hoped that she had said the right thing.

She gave some thought as to what to wear for the tea-party. Most of the people who were coming were considerably older than herself, and to emphasise the difference in years might create a bad impression. She chose a silvery grey jersey dress with a pale patterned scarf at the neck, elegant and simple, and then went to the drawing-room to await her guests.

The tea-party was a success. Wolke had made fairy cakes, cut minuscule cucumber sandwiches, and together she and Trixie had made a Victoria sponge light as air. Her guests, enjoying these dainties, told her all there was to know about life at the university and the medical school. 'Now Krijn is a married man,' Mevrouw van Vliet told her, 'we no longer need to worry about him,' and at Trixie's enquiring look she added, 'When he was a bachelor we felt it our duty to make it possible for him to meet as many new people as we could arrange—a man needs a wife.' She beamed at Trixie. 'But now he has found one for himself, and, if I may say so, a delightful bride. We are all agreed about that.'

Trixie thanked her, rather pink in the face, reflecting that Krijn's drastic action in marrying her had certainly been the right answer to escaping from the well-meaning ladies' efforts to marry him off. At least he had chosen a wife for himself.

She waved the last of them on their way home and went back to the drawing-room, to find Krijn sitting in his chair. He came to meet her as she crossed the room. 'I had tea in my study,' he told her. 'The afternoon went off well?'

'How long have you been home?'

'An hour.' He gave her a thoughtful look. 'They were kind, Beatrice?'

'Oh, yes, and so friendly.' She smiled suddenly. 'They explained that they had all been so anxious about you because you weren't married. It seems they tried their hardest to find you a wife...'

He gave a crack of laughter. 'Oh, indeed they did; endless dinners, invitations to have a drink and meet a niece or an old friend's daughter.'

'Was it as bad as that in London too?'

'Yes. Now, about the people we must invite for drinks while we are there—quite a few from the hospital, your friends too, of course, and I have a number of acquaintances.'

'How many?'

'Altogether around thirty, I suppose. Mies and Gladys can cope; Gladys has a sister who will come in and help.'

'Oh, it's something you do each year?'

'If I'm in England, yes. Of course on Christmas Day I go to Timothy's to carve a turkey and do a round of the wards...'

'Yes. I saw you last Christmas.' She had been a first-year student nurse then, on the children's ward and de-tailed to feed some of the toddlers, and he had wandered round with Sister, stopping to sit on the cots and admire the toys the children had had. She hadn't known who he was but her friends had told her and she had glimpsed him from time to time until she had gone to work on Women's Medical and saw him regularly. She supposed with hindsight that she had fallen in love with him then and never known it.

'I shall be at the hospital all day tomorrow,' he told her. 'St Nikolaas will arrive on his white horse with

Zwarte Piet directly after lunch. I'll fetch you about one o'clock; you'll have time to see him before you need to be in the village. He usually arrives there about four o'clock.'

'Not the same one?'

'No. No. Holland is littered with him, he'll be in every town and village and the remarkable thing is that the small children don't realise it.'

She was really all ready for him when he got home after her early lunch. It was still very cold and she had got into her new winter coat, hunter's green mohair, and pulled on her chestnut-brown leather boots. She had arranged a matching velvet cap on her neat head of hair and collected her Gucci handbag and gloves, hoping that she would present the right image to anyone she might meet at the hospital.

Krijn got out of the car and opened her door, sweeping a pile of papers on to the back seat as he did so, whistled to Samson, mooning at the door to get in too, and drove off, casting a sidelong glance at Trixie as he did so. 'Very nice. I like the thing on your head. You are to meet the *directrice* and the *directeur* before we greet the Sint.'

'Oh, will there be a lot of people there?'

'Every single soul who can be spared from the hospital. He shakes hands with everyone and then goes round the wards. I'll bring you back before he starts, for it takes some time. I should be home around six o'clock. I'd like you to stay in the village until I come for you.'

'I can walk back, it's only ten minutes or so—I'll take a torch.'

'I prefer to collect you, Beatrice.'

'Well, all right. I'll wait.'

They were at the hospital by now and he parked the car in the space reserved for the consultants and walked her to the entrance. There were quite a number of people standing around, despite the cold, but inside it was comfortably warm and the dignitaries of the hospital were standing in groups, chatting. There were nurses too and medical students making a cheerful hum of talk. Krijn had taken her arm and was leading her to where several people stood together.

'The reception committee,' he told her softly and introduced her to the *directrice* and the *directeur*, who made small talk in English and introduced her to the others there. She had already met some of them at the dinner party; Mevrouw van Vliet was there and several of the ladies who had come to tea on the previous day. They surrounded her at once, vying with each other to explain what was to happen next, and Krijn gave her a smile and went away to talk to two elderly gentlemen with handsome beards.

The Sint's approach was heralded by distant cheering and presently he was seen, riding his white horse with Zwarte Piet walking beside him. He dismounted at the hospital entrance, waved to the crowds which had gathered, and made his stately way inside. Here he was greeted by the *directeur*, shook hands with the welcoming committee and proceeded with great dignity to the wards.

Trixie would quite liked to have gone too, but Krijn tapped her on the shoulder. 'I'll drive you back home,' he told her in a voice which brooked no argument.

She said with a trace of peevishness, 'I should have liked to stay... I don't need to be in the village until four o'clock.'

To which remark he made no reply.

There was a car parked outside the door of the house. Krijn drew up beside it and opened Trixie's door so that she saw it before anything else. It was a Mini, dark blue and gleaming with newness. Across its bonnet was a broad ribbon with 'For Beatrice from St Nikolaas' printed upon it.

She stood goggling at it. 'For me—a car? Krijn...'

'Don't look at me, my dear, I'm not St Nikolaas.'

'Yes, but you—that is—— Oh, Krijn, thank you very much. What a lovely present.'

'I'll let the Sint know,' he told her gravely. 'Get Rabo to put it in the garage for you.'

'Oh, but could I drive down to the village...?'

He shook his head. 'I shall pick you up around six o'clock.'

He got back into the Bentley. 'I'll see you then.'

She went indoors, rather put out to be met by Rabo. 'I will walk down with you, *mevrouw*. There is a basket of sweets and biscuits, too heavy for you.'

Almost everyone in the village had come to see St Nikolaas's arrival. He was punctual, looking, behind his disguising whiskers and flowing robes, remarkably like Mijnheer Blind the butcher. For the children, at least he was magic and everyone sang a welcoming song before he went around handing out the little packages Trixie had packed so carefully.

He went away again presently, attended by Zwarte Piet, and the children were handed oranges and sweets and little cakes and were borne home, leaving Mevrouw Kraan and the butcher's wife and Trixie to clear away the papers and the half-eaten buns and sweets. They had finished when Krijn arrived, stayed a few minutes to talk to the ladies and offer them a bottle of wine each before sweeping Trixie into the car.

Back in the house once more, he said, 'Shall we have coffee in the drawing-room? Or perhaps you would rather have tea... It has been a busy day.'

So they sat, he with his coffee-pot, she with her tea-tray, and mulled over their day, and presently they had dinner and went back to the drawing-room again. Mevrouw van der Brink-Schaaksma telephoned during the evening wanting to know what Trixie thought of St Nikolaas and wishing them a pleasant journey back to England. 'We shall all see you on Old Year's Day,' she observed. 'We shall look forward to that.'

Trixie wasn't sure if she looked forward to it or not. The next morning she spent some time with Wolke and Rabo while they explained everything which had to be done. 'Each year it is the same,' said Rabo. 'Tradition, you say, yes? But do not worry, *mevrouw*, we shall prepare everything while you are away, if you will tell Wolke what you wish to be eaten...'

They settled on the menus, which bedrooms should be used and arrangements for the smaller children. The nurseries were to be opened and aired and Pibbe had a nanny who would look after all the children and sleep close by. Trixie heaved a sigh of relief knowing that Rabo and Wolke would see that she did the right thing, and went to her room to get into something wearable for her visit to Mevrouw van Vliet.

She was going to drive herself into Leiden. She hadn't got her full Dutch licence yet but Rabo would sit beside her in case they encountered a police patrol. Besides, she was secretly relieved to have him there; she had to get used to driving on the wrong side of the road...

The afternoon went well. She drank pale milkless tea and ate *speculaas* and listened politely to the advice the ladies there poured into her ears. That they meant it kindly was evident; they were anxious that she should slip into her appointed role of consultant's wife with the least effort and she was grateful to them. They clustered round her wishing her a happy Christmas and voicing their pleasure at the idea of seeing her again so soon after the festivities. She looked around at their kind faces and realised that she no longer felt a stranger, something she tried to explain to Krijn that evening. It was a pity that the phone should ring just as she was making herself clear and by the time he had had a lengthy conversation with whoever was on the other end there was no point in continuing; besides, he went to his study shortly after and since she had nothing better to do she went upstairs and started to pack.

They travelled to England on the night ferry to Harwich so that the professor could do a day's work before he went. There was a hint of snow in the air when they left and the country around the house looked bleak. Trixie felt decidedly sad as they drove away, leaving Rabo, Wolke and an unhappy Samson on the doorstep. She said suddenly, 'I'm glad we're coming back. Do you live here more than in London, Krijn?'

He glanced at her. 'Yes, but I have wondered sometimes if I should do rather less work in England. It is so easy and quick to fly over, I could rearrange my work. Until now I have never bothered about it.'

'Now have you changed your mind?'

'Not entirely.'

With that she had to be satisfied. She longed to question him further but he spoke so seldom about himself and she was afraid that any curiosity on her part might spoil the easygoing friendship existing between them.

There was a nasty cold rain falling when they got to Harwich and Trixie was feeling queasy after a rough crossing. She gave Krijn a reproachful look when she was asked cheerfully, 'Breakfast, don't you think? I have no appointments until this afternoon.'

Trixie said in a hollow voice, 'I don't think I'm hungry...'

He was driving through the town and then pulled up before a hotel. 'Tea—a pot of tea and some toast—just to please me.'

She felt better after the first cup of tea and ate some toast while the professor, with due concern for her qualms, contented himself with porridge, toast and marmalade and a pot of coffee. She certainly felt better after more tea and toast, and got back into the car looking almost her normal self. 'You were quite right,' she told him, 'I do feel much better.' Indeed, she began to talk cheerfully about their stay in London. 'It will be nice to see some of my friends at Timothy's. You won't mind?'

'My dear Beatrice, of course I don't mind. All I ask is that you keep our social activities to a minimum. Did you write to your aunt?'

'Yes, but there hasn't been time for her to reply. Probably she won't.'

'That is one invitation I should like you to accept if it is offered.'

She said, 'Very well,' and wondered why he was so anxious to see her aunt again. For her part she really didn't mind if she didn't see her again, although she would like to see Uncle William. She fell silent, wondering if she should go and see Margaret, and since Krijn had nothing to say she occupied herself in planning Christmas. A quiet one, she guessed, but there was no reason why they shouldn't have a proper Christmas dinner and even have a Christmas tree and presents...

The outskirts of London closed in on them and the professor slowed his pace. 'We will go straight to the house,' he observed. 'Mies will have an early lunch ready for us. You will be all right this afternoon? I should be back in the early evening.'

She assured him that she would be fine; there was the unpacking to see to and she and Mies could have a talk. 'Will you be working every day until Christmas?' she wanted to know.

He smiled. 'Not every day—three, four times a week, perhaps, at the hospital, but I have a number of patients to see at my rooms and I may have to go to Bristol and Birmingham. I'm sure we shall take time to do some Christmas shopping. I must leave you to see to the cards and so on. Get them printed—we shall need about a hundred. Mrs Grey has always done them for me, but you will take that over, won't you? And presents, I'll give you a list, that will leave her free to get my letters done and all the notes typed up.'

Trixie said, 'Yes, of course,' meekly, reflecting that she need not worry about not having enough to keep her occupied; she would have more than enough.

Their welcome back home was a warm one. Mies flung the door wide with Gladys hovering in the background and Caesar himself, full of joy, barked his head off. Even Gumbie came silently to stare at them and wreathe himself round their legs.

'Coffee,' said Mies. 'I bring it at once to the drawing-room. And such a good lunch I have prepared. *Mevrouw*, you will wish to get out of your outdoor things.'

She bustled round, breaking into Dutch when her English failed her. Trixie went up to her room and

washed her face and did her hair, and when she got back
to the drawing-room it was to find the coffee-tray set on
the little table by her usual chair and the professor sitting
on the other side of the blazing fire, Caesar lying across
his shoes and Gumbie on the arm of his chair. He had
a pile of letters on the table beside him and glanced up
briefly as she went in. 'Forgive me if I don't get up,' he
said, 'Caesar has me pinned by the feet and I shall drop
this lot. There are several letters for us both and one for
you—no, here is another with a Dutch postmark...'

She took them from him and sat down to open them.
Aunt Alice bidding them to dine with a few friends. 'Less
than a week away,' said Trixie. 'Will that be all right?'

He nodded. 'Remind me.' He bowed his head over the
letter in his hand and she opened the second letter. It
was from Andre, regretting that he hadn't seen her before
they left Holland, wishing them a happy Christmas and
declaring, rather fulsomely, that he would miss her, and
looked forward to getting to know her really well when
they returned.

She glanced up and found Krijn's eyes upon her and
said quickly, 'It's from Andre—he's sorry he didn't see
us to say goodbye and he hopes we'll all have a happy
Christmas and—and he's looking forward to seeing us
when we get back.'

'Very civil of him.' The professor didn't tell her that
he had seen his cousin on the day before they had left
Holland. Beatrice, he could see, was feeling uncomfort-
able; it would never do to make her more so by telling
her that. 'He's good company.'

'Yes—yes, he is...' She was interrupted by Gladys
coming in with a sheaf of flowers in Cellophane and tied
with ribbon. 'This came, *mevrouw*—it's for you.'

Trixie took the bouquet: freesias, roses, carnations and lilac. She peeped at Krijn to see if he had known about it, but he was looking blandly at her and her forlorn hope that he had sent them died. There was a note on the card: 'To Trixie—sweets to the sweet. Andre.'

She went slowly red. 'It's from Andre. I suppose it's a kind of welcome-home gift. How kind of him.'

The professor's voice was as bland as his face. 'Most thoughtful,' he observed. 'I dare say he thought that you might feel homesick for Holland.'

Trixie gave a thankful silent sigh; Krijn didn't mind and she had no reason to feel guilty. 'Well, you know, I do miss Holland, although I ought not to—I'm English, I mean, aren't I?'

He said comfortably, 'I dare say you will settle down here for a few weeks.' He got to his feet, hampered by Caesar, who had fallen asleep. 'I must do some telephoning. Is lunch at one o'clock?'

'Yes, if that suits you.'

'Admirably.' He went away to his study, but it was quite some time before he reached for the phone. Trixie's small flushed face and her faint air of guilt had given him something to think about. The trouble was, he wasn't sure why he needed to think about her in the first place.

Trixie, left to herself, went in search of a vase, arranged the flowers and burnt the card. It had been kind of Andre to write to her and send her flowers but quite unnecessary. She supposed that she would have to thank him, but she could do that when she sent their cards before Christmas. She felt relieved at having solved the problem, and picked up the bundle of letters Krijn had left for her. Cards mostly and several invitations. He had scrawled 'no' across most of them, leaving her, she

supposed rather crossly, to think up suitable excuses. She
was to accept an invitation from the hospital for the
annual ball and four or five cocktail parties and a dinner
with one of the consultants and his wife, and Aunt Alice,
of course.

Over lunch, lovingly presented by Mies, he gave her
the list of cards to send, suggested a date for their own
cocktail party, assured her that he was quite sure that
she could produce suitable excuses for most of their invitations and presently went away. 'Enjoy your afternoon,' he begged her, and patted her shoulder, leaving
her with the prospect of a few hours at the little desk in
the sitting-room. I shall probably get writer's cramp, she
thought gloomily.

By the time Gladys came in with the tea-tray, she had
ordered the invitations for their own party, written ac-
ceptances of those invitations which Krijn wished to go
to and started on the diplomatic refusals of the others.
She was quite pleased with her afternoon's work and
made haste to tell him so when he got back shortly
afterwards.

He answered her with his usual courtesy but she could
see that his mind was elsewhere. 'Did something go
wrong? Do you want to talk about it?' she asked.

'Do you remember the patient I told you of? That
patient with exophthalmos? We spent the day by the
sea...'

Of course she remembered—that was the exact
moment when she had fallen in love with him. 'Yes, I
remember...'

'There are now cardiovascular symptoms...'

Trixie sat, patiently listening, loving the sound of his
voice while not attending overmuch to what he was
saying. That just talking about it was giving him the

opportunity to mull over the problem was obvious; she wasn't surprised when he paused and said, 'Ah, I believe I see what can be done. I must ring my registrar. She should be admitted again at once. I shall telephone her husband and arrange for her to go to Timothy's this evening.'

He paused long enough at the door to say, 'If I'm not back don't wait dinner, Beatrice.'

She wasn't surprised about that either.

She went to confer with Mies presently, for she guessed that the good soul had taken great pains to give them a magnificent meal, and she had been right.

'If we could have dinner a little later?' she suggested. 'And if we have a good excuse the professor won't know that we've rearranged it. What could hinder you so that we don't sit down until, say, eight o'clock?'

'I shall think of something,' declared Mies. 'Do not worry, *mevrouw*. It is a good idea. He eats too many of the sandwiches in that hospital and when he returns late he is no longer hungry for my good food.'

'We'll change that,' said Trixie firmly. 'It's time he stopped being a bachelor.'

Mies looked coy. 'But that he no longer is, *mevrouw*. You will teach him the good habits, I think.'

'Oh, rather,' said Trixie, and went back to the drawing-room to let Gumbie in from the garden. Caesar had gone with Krijn, sitting proudly beside him in the car.

Fortune favoured their scheme; the long-case clock was striking eight as Krijn let himself into his home, and Trixie met him with a cheerful, 'Oh, good. We haven't had dinner yet—Mies accidently burnt the rice. It's *poulet chasseur*—it's almost ready. You've time for a drink?'

The professor cast down his coat, took his bag to his study and joined her by the fire. 'I've never known Mies burn anything...'

'I dare say she was a bit excited at us coming today. I'm sure everything else will be delicious.' She declined his offer of a drink and asked, 'Did things turn out as you wanted them to?'

'Yes. I think eventually everything will be all right. Have you had a quiet afternoon?'

He didn't really want to know, she felt sure. She thought of the pile of envelopes waiting to be posted and said that yes, it had been very quiet and pleasant.

They dined presently on watercress soup, the *poulet chasseur* with its accompaniment of faultlessly cooked rice, and one of Mies's mouthwatering puddings to follow, a chestnut soufflé with a chocolate cream sauce.

The meal was rather a silent one; Trixie tried various topics of conversation and although Krijn answered her readily she guessed that his brain was occupied with some problem so that presently she became silent, and when they went to drink their coffee in the drawing-room she took up her tapestry and became absorbed in it, unaware that she made a charming picture sitting in the pink glow of the table-lamp at her elbow, her mousy head bent over her work. The professor, looking at her from his chair, found his usually well-disciplined thoughts wandering so that very shortly he took himself off to his study to busy himself until long after midnight planning his work schedule for the next few weeks. Naturally enough, when he at last went back to the drawing-room Trixie had gone to bed. He checked the locks and bolts, turned out the lights and went to bed himself. He caught sight of Andre's flowers, tastefully arranged in a vase in the hall, as he went upstairs, and he frowned.

Andre was all right, he supposed, although not particularly liked by him, but the fellow had no right to send Beatrice flowers and notes. She was, he reminded himself, a kind and sensible girl, anxious to please and touchingly trusting with little or no experience of men. A bunch of flowers and a letter or two and she might imagine herself interested in Andre. The professor, who, if he needed to send flowers, got Mrs Grey to order them and give him the bill and hadn't written a love-letter for the best part of fifteen years, sighed. He trusted Beatrice; they had made a bargain and he knew that she would keep to it, but he didn't want her to be hurt. He decided that he would get tickets for some show. He must remember to ask her what she would like to see.

Trixie slipped into the professor's well-ordered days without much effort. She was kept busy, what with the Christmas cards, presents for the friends at Timothy's, the planning of their own party and visits—prompted by kindly curiosity, she felt sure—of the wives of Krijn's colleagues at Timothy's. They went, several days after their arrival in England, to a cocktail party at the hospital. She wore an amber crêpe dress which made the most of her pretty figure and Krijn gave her a thick gold chain necklace to wear with it. 'I bought it to give to you at our wedding but it slipped my mind,' he told her. She thanked him quietly.

It was strange to meet on an equal footing the senior medical staff she had never even spoken to before, although she had seen them dozens of times on the wards. Several of the older ward sisters were there too, among them Sister Snell, being very polite, eyeing her clothes and her Italian shoes and the gold chain and longing, Trixie thought with an inward giggle, to tell her to go and tidy the sluice. Krijn had behaved exactly as any newly-wed girl would wish a husband to behave. Of course his beautiful manners wouldn't allow him to be anything else, and he had looked at her once or twice, really looked almost as though he had never seen her before.

Beautiful clothes make a difference, she told herself as she jumped into bed that night. I'm a lucky girl. She cried herself to sleep.

They went shopping together once to choose presents for Mies and Gladys and to get something to take back to Rabo and Wolke. They had wandered in and out of Liberty's and Krijn had bought her a scarf she happened to admire before choosing a quilted dressing-gown for Mies and a leather handbag for Gladys. 'Mrs Grey has always chosen something for the ward sisters,' he observed. 'She is only too glad to hand that task over to you.'

'How many and which ones?'

'Ah, now, let me see—the medical ward sisters and the children's ward sisters and the theatre sisters—Matron too, of course. Half a dozen bottles of wine to the path lab and a crate of beer for the housemen...'

'I do not know how to buy crates of beer,' said Trixie, 'or for that matter bottles of wine.'

'No, no, you have no need, I'll see to that. But I have neither the time nor the knowledge for all those women.'

'Flower arrangements,' said Trixie. 'Let us find a florist and order them. Women love having flowers.' She wished she hadn't said that, thinking guiltily about the flowers Andre had sent, although she had no reason to feel guilty.

She peeped at Krijn but his face remained placid and all he said was, 'Then let us see to it immediately.'

The flowers were chosen, each arrangement different, and, the astronomical bill having been paid, they turned their attention to finding something for Rabo and Wolke. 'A tea-set,' declared Trixie, once more in Liberty's. 'Something bone china and made in England.'

So a pleasant half-hour was spent choosing something exactly right and if the professor was bored or impatient he concealed it very well. It was when they arrived back home that she said thoughtfully, 'I should think that a bottle of champagne with Matron's flowers might be a good idea.'

The professor, who believed in distributing champagne with a lavish hand at Christmas and had done so for years, observed that it was a splendid idea and he would most certainly do that. To tell her that he had done so for years would never do; just lately he found an increasing reluctance to say anything which might bring the look of a hurt child to her small, unassuming face.

At breakfast on the day on which they were bidden to dine with Aunt Alice and Uncle William, he looked up from his letters to ask, 'Will it be black tie this evening?'

'Yes, it's on the invitation. There will be other guests.'

She was quite taken aback when he asked, 'What are you wearing, Beatrice?'

'I thought perhaps the grey...'

'A charming dress, but didn't you buy something pink in den Haag? I seem to remember it. Have you got it with you?'

'Well, yes, I have. Won't it be too—too noticeable?'

'My dear Beatrice, it is Christmas and party time! It will be exactly right.'

So she wore the 'pink' dress, a lovely soft apricot, chiffon over silk with long tight sleeves and an artfully cut bodice which made the very best of her curves. She wore the gold chain with it and when Krijn came home that evening he handed her a small velvet box. 'An early Christmas present,' he told her, and when she opened it there were earrings inside, gold, discreetly dangling and set with sapphires.

She held them in her hands, staring down at them. 'Thank you, Krijn,' she said at last. 'They're beautiful—I shall wear them tonight; they go so well with the chain and the ring.'

She hooked them into her ears and went to admire them in the big maple-framed mirror in the drawing-room and then turned round to say again, 'Thank you, they're quite lovely.'

The professor was watching her from the door. 'Good.' He sounded uninterested and she felt a surge of disappointment as he went away.

Aunt Alice's house was brilliantly lit when they reached it and there was another new maid to answer the door. This time their coats and wraps were taken from them and they were announced at the drawing-room door. There were ten or twelve people there and they all looked round as they went in. Trixie smiled composedly in a general manner and made her way to where her aunt and uncle were standing. She knew now why Krijn had been so insistent upon her wearing the pink dress and why he had given her the earrings; the last time they had come Aunt Alice had treated them with discourtesy and he hadn't forgotten. Her small chin went up and she said clearly, 'How are you, Aunt Alice, and you, Uncle? Of course you know Krijn.'

Aunt Alice went an ugly red and murmured a greeting; it was Uncle William who took her hand and kissed her cheek. 'Why, my dear, how well you look, and how pretty.' He shook Krijn's hand and then led them round the room introducing them. Halfway round the big room they came face to face with Margaret. Trixie said hello in her soft voice and her cousin eyed her up and down.

'Oh, hello.' Her smile was unfriendly although it changed to delight as she greeted Krijn. She tucked an arm into his and said sweetly, 'You're taking me in to dinner. You can tell me how you've managed to transform my plain little cousin.' She paused and added lightly, 'Clothes do help, of course.'

He moved a little way away so that she had to take her hand from his arm. He was smiling but the cool look he gave her from head to toe was all the answer he needed to give. He took Trixie's hand in his and said blandly, 'I see Colonel Vosper over there, my dear—we must have a word with him.'

He smiled at Margaret but his eyes were hard, so that she said hastily, 'Of course I was only joking...'

'Why, of course you were,' he agreed silkily.

The evening seemed to go on forever. 'What a waste of an evening,' said Trixie as they drove home.

'Certainly not, Beatrice. Your aunt now knows just what kind of a girl you are—not a mouselike little creature treated as a poor relation, but a young woman who can hold her own, who dresses well and looks charming.'

Trixie turned to gape at him. 'Krijn—did you think of me like that, as a...mouselike poor relation?'

He glanced sideways at her astonished face and smiled. 'No. I can't remember what I thought, but certainly not that. When we get home we will open a bottle of champagne and drown our disastrous dinner. Your aunt's cook must have a grudge against us all—badly cooked food smothered in nasty sauces. I shall get Mies to make us some sandwiches.'

So they spent the remainder of the evening sitting comfortably by the drawing-room fire with Gumbie on Trixie's lap and Caesar in his usual spot by the professor's feet, eating a pile of delicious sandwiches Mies offered and drinking the champagne he had fetched up from the cellar.

Trixie hadn't been so happy for a long time. In bed she didn't waste time thinking about the dinner party but allowed her thoughts to dwell on the couple of hours she had spent with Krijn. It had been like someone opening a door just a crack so that she might see what being married was really like.

CHAPTER EIGHT

THE next couple of days were filled from morning to night and Trixie saw very little of Krijn. He had regular visits to Timothy's and his afternoons were frequently taken up with private patients. In the evenings he worked at his book or dictated his letters ready for Mrs Grey in the morning. Trixie, having dispatched the cards, conferred with Mies and seen to the small chores which fell to her lot around the house, took coffee or tea with those of Krijn's colleagues' wives who had invited her and got rather adept at evading invitations to dinner for them both, allowing their would-be hostesses to assume that, being newly-wed, they wished, for the time being at least, to spend what leisure they had together. She bore the knowing looks and little smiles with good grace, only wishing that that were the reason.

He found time to go shopping with her once more, this time in the morning, to Harrods to find presents for his family; a handbag for his mother, scent for his sisters and Chivas Regal malt whisky for his father, and over coffee he observed, 'What shall we give my horde of nephews and nieces?'

'Well, let's see—there are seven, aren't there? Six boys and one girl. She might like Little Grey Rabbit, I saw her as we came through the toy department—very nicely dressed with a shopping basket—just the thing...' She didn't see his little smile, but went on, 'As for the boys, they're more difficult. Perhaps Lego—there's one with blocks to be hammered into a board. They're almost

three, aren't they? And Reka's boy—is he old enough
for one of those cars you can drive by remote control?'

'Little boys are always old enough for cars,' observed
the professor.

'Yes, well, that leaves Soeske's three boys.'

'A train set—they can all play with it.' He put down
his cup. 'If you're ready then let's go and get it.'

Half an hour later Trixie watched the professor write
a cheque for what seemed to her to be a complete miniature railway system of the United Kingdom, together with
sundry stations, bridges, signal boxes and miles of miniature track. He and the salesman had been completely
absorbed in assembling it, something which had entailed
trying out each piece of rolling-stock over every inch of
rail.

Trixie, watching the professor's absorbed face, loved
him so much that it hurt.

They bought the rest of the toys and then went to
Claridge's for lunch where Trixie ate delicious food in
elegant surroundings with the enjoyment of a child
having a treat. Krijn, watching her pleasure, found,
rather to his surprise, that he was enjoying himself. As
for Trixie, she wondered hopefully if their morning
together might be the forerunner of several.

She was to be disappointed, for the rest of that day
and for the next two days she saw hardly anything of
him and if it hadn't been for the hospital ball on the day
after that she would probably not have seen him then
either. He found time to ask her if she needed a new
dress for the occasion, left a wad of notes by her plate
and later that day phoned to remind her to be ready to
leave the house by eight o'clock. 'We shall be dining
first,' he told her belatedly. 'Some of the hospital
committee...'

'Where?'

He sounded impatient. 'In the hospital; we shall go from there to the big hall. The dancing starts at half-past eight but it is usual for us to get there an hour or so later.' He rang off, presumably to concentrate his brilliant mind upon the intricacies of the glandular system.

Despite her resolve to be a good wife, Trixie was put out—the ball of the year and barely two days' notice. True, she had brought a dress with her, but was it grand enough for such an important occasion? Besides, she wished very much to impress Staff Nurse Bennett...

The notes were for a very satisfying sum; she took herself off to Knightsbridge and searched for something suitable. It took her a little while to find it, but it had been worth the search. Organza, roses on a pale green background over a silk slip exactly matching the soft pink of the flowers and to go with it pink satin slippers and a small golden-mesh bag to hang over one wrist. She had packed her gossamer fine cashmere wrap; all she needed to do was to wash her hair, and go to bed that night with a face cream guaranteed to do wonders to her complexion.

At breakfast Krijn looked up from his letters for long enough to ask, 'All ready for this evening? I'm going to Birmingham this morning but I should be back by seven at the latest.'

She didn't think that he had heard her when she assured him that she was quite ready, but he did look up when she suggested that he might like a few sandwiches and coffee when he got back.

'Thank you, I'll be glad of them. Make a good tea, Beatrice; the wine tends to flow at these functions...'

She eyed him coldly. 'Are you suggesting that I might drink more than I should?'

He had got up ready to go. 'Lord, no, but champagne on empty insides wreaks havoc.' He dropped a hand on her shoulder. 'I'll see you this evening. I've left a phone number on my desk.'

She was dressed and in the drawing-room, working away at the tapestry, when he got back. She heard him come into the house but she stayed where she was; she had arranged herself in a chair not too near the fire, with a pink-shaded lamp at her elbow and her dress spread out around her. She wasn't a conceited girl but she thought that she looked rather nice to come home to and she hoped that Krijn might think the same.

He came into the room with a book in his hand, bringing a good deal of the cold outdoors with him. His 'Hello' was cheerful and brisk and beyond a glance in her direction he didn't pause as he crossed the room to his chair. Indeed, to a close observer, it seemed as though he was deliberately not looking at her.

Trixie swallowed disappointment, stabbed viciously at her tapestry and enquired as to his day. 'There are sand-wiches on the table beside you—Mies bought them in not five minutes ago.'

She could be forgiven for the slight tartness in her voice.

He went away presently to change and she sat forcing herself to calm down; he was tired, she told herself, and probably he was still thinking about a patient; after all, he had made it quite clear that his work was more im-portant to him than anything else and for him the evening ahead was very likely a waste of time. By the time he came downstairs again she looked the picture of serenity.

She hadn't been looking forward to the dinner party but it turned out to be a very convivial affair; she was seated between two of the senior consultants who called her the little lady and plied her with wine which she carefully sipped, and, although it was an official dinner, since it was Christmas it quickly turned into a jolly occasion. Krijn, sitting opposite her at the long table, with a formidable lady on either side of him, smiled at her whenever their eyes met, and she was able to study him at her leisure. For once, he didn't look absent-minded and it was obvious that his dinner companions were enjoying themselves; the next time he smiled at her over the tastefully arranged centre-piece she gave him a cool look.

The ball was in full swing when they got to it, and, without a word, he swung her on to the dance-floor. 'That was a nasty look you gave me at dinner,' he said into her ear. 'Have I done something or not done something or not said something and put you out?'

'Nothing at all,' said Trixie into his shirtfront. 'What a delightful evening this is.' She sounded frosty.

'Delightful, and I am being complimented right, left and centre on having such a charming bride.'

She said, 'Pah!' into his shirtfront again, and he laughed and held her rather more tightly than was necessary.

She danced the whole evening and in between she sought out her friends and even came face to face with Staff Nurse Bennett, who said snappily, 'I suppose I have to call you *mevrouw* . . .'

'Not if you don't want to,' said Trixie. 'I'm still me, you know.'

The last waltz was struck up and since there was no sign of Krijn she was about to float away on the arm of her dinner partner when she was whisked away by the professor with a brief apology.

'I hadn't forgotten,' he told her, and he sounded as though he was laughing. 'But I had to have a word with Johnson. Have you enjoyed yourself?'

'Yes, thank you.' She had closed her eyes and was pretending that he loved her and that he would never let her go again; there was no harm in a little daydreaming.

It was almost two o'clock in the morning by the time they got home. She stood uncertainly in the hall and he asked, 'Would you like a drink?'

She refused in a quiet little voice, cast her wrap down on a chair and started for the staircase. Her 'goodnight' was almost a whisper.

The professor, standing by the door, watching her, caught her up as she reached the first stair. 'You are so pretty in your lovely dress and your eyes are so bright and shining. I don't want you to think that I have only just noticed that. You were like a picture this evening when I came home, sitting by the fire in the lamplight...'

He swooped suddenly and kissed her quite roughly and then a second time with a gentleness that set her heart pounding against her ribs. 'Oh!' said Trixie, and slipped away from his hands on her shoulders and raced up the stairs, not quite knowing what she was doing or why.

He watched her go without a word, smiling a little, and then, with the faithful but sleepy Caesar at his heels, went into his study. For a little while at least, he had no desire to sleep.

She felt shy about seeing him at breakfast the next morning, but she need not have worried; there he sat, looking exactly as he always looked, and his good morning was uttered in a casual friendly voice. With a slightly heightened colour she sat down opposite him and drank her coffee, and almost dropped the cup when he said, 'You look just as pretty this morning, Beatrice.'

The pretty colour in her cheeks deepened. 'But I'm not pretty,' she pointed out.

'Beauty is in the eye of the beholder.' He cast down the papers he was studying. 'Shall we have a day out? Shall we go back to the sea and have lunch at the Ship Inn?'

She stared across the table at him; his sleepy eyes were open and there was a look in them which made her catch her breath. 'Oh, Krijn, there's nothing——' She was interrupted by Gladys, coming into the room burdened by a large basket filled with red roses and extravagantly beribboned.

'These have just come, *mevrouw*—special messenger—and there's a note.'

She put the basket down by Trixie's chair and went away, casting a coy look at the professor as she went. 'There's a husband for you,' she told Mies. 'Red roses and all.'

Trixie cast a smiling look at Krijn and opened the envelope. It was a brief note inside: 'Remember me? Red roses to remind you, Andre.'

She looked at Krijn. The lids had drooped over his eyes once more, his face was bland and she was quite sure that he was angry despite the mildness of his expression. 'It's from Andre,' she told him.

'Saying it with flowers?' He sounded only mildly interested, so that she felt safe in repeating the note's contents.

'Do you need reminding, Beatrice?' he enquired still placidly.

'Well, of course not.' She wasn't thinking of Andre but of the nice old house and Samson; Wolke bustling around and Rabo smoothing her path for her. 'How could I forget?' She looked down at the note on the table, not seeing it, lost for a moment in a daydream where Krijn and Schaakslot and being kissed were all nicely muddled up together, and was startled from it by the professor getting to his feet and pushing back the chair.

'I think that after all we must postpone a day out. I had quite forgotten that Mrs Grey has made a number of appointments for me which cannot be cancelled.'

She lifted a disappointed face. 'Perhaps in a day or two—it's almost Christmas...'

'Ah, yes. I can arrange to go back to Holland a couple of days after Boxing Day. You will like that?'

'Oh, yes, of course, that is, if you want to. But you'll be home here for Christmas? All day, I mean.'

'I did tell you that I shall go to Timothy's to carve a turkey and go round the wards?'

'Oh, yes, of course. May I come too?'

'By all means.' He went to the door. 'I shan't be home until some time after tea.'

She sat very still after he had gone, not in the least taken in by his bland manner. He was furiously angry and it had to do with the roses. It was silly of Andre to pester her but surely that wouldn't make Krijn so savagely angry? She *surely* must have said something... Now, if he had been in love with her she could have understood that. She sat up very straight; could that be it? Could he have fallen in love with her by some miraculous chance, and if he had what could she do about it?

Nothing for the moment, she decided; for one thing it might be wishful thinking on her part and surely she would know one way or another before long? Perhaps she had imagined his rage; after all, there had been no outward signs of it.

There were no signs of rage as the professor went on his rounds at Timothy's, indeed he was remarkably and uncharacteristically alert, so that the ward sisters and students and housemen remarked upon it. It was so unusual to see him without a book tucked under his arm, or to find him coming into a ward exactly on time and that after only a few hours' sleep.

Sister Snell, discussing him with Staff Nurse Bennett, remarked waspishly, 'It must be because he's married. What he can see in her I can't think, although I must say she looked stunning last night.'

The subject of their conversation was wandering through the Brompton Arcade, searching for a present for Krijn; she had left it until the last moment hoping that she might be able to discover what he would like but he had given her no clue, so that she was forced to inspect each shop in turn in the hope of seeing something he might be glad to have. There was plenty to choose from: ties, scarves and cashmere sweaters, cufflinks and leather briefcases. She decided that he was a man who liked to choose his own ties—richly sombre and silk—and he had everything else. She wanted it to be something he would use every day, something to remind him of her. Finally she bought a silver pocket knife, small and light and incorporating every gadget he might be called upon to use. He would most likely never use it.

She took it home and wrapped it up carefully, hesitating over the card to go with it. In the end she wrote, 'From Beatrice to Krijn, a happy Christmas,' and put it away in a drawer in her room.

Almost everyone who had been invited to the drinks party had accepted the invitation; Trixie spent the rest of the day and the following one in getting ready for it. While Mies saw to the food and Gladys saw to the preparation of the drawing-room, Trixie decorated a Christmas tree and set it in the hall and then saw to the flower arrangements around the house, holly and Christmas roses and hyacinths. She then firmly closed the drawing-room door, and, when Krijn got home that evening, asked him diffidently if he would mind sitting in the small sitting-room behind the dining-room. 'Because the drawing-room is ready for the party tomorrow.'

He had forgotten about it. For a brief moment she felt deep sympathy with the women who had wanted to marry him; she could imagine any number of engagements he must have forgotten or overlooked during his years of being a bachelor and the well-meaning ladies would have been only too glad to take him in hand. Something she wanted to do very badly herself, but the whole idea of his marrying her was to make sure that he wouldn't be bothered with a social life. This party, she supposed, arranging a miniature Father Christmas on a sleigh in the centre of the table which would hold the food, was to be the one and only social occasion, save for the ball which had been absolutely unavoidable anyway, before they returned to Holland. So it must be a success . . .

As it turned out, it didn't matter about not sitting in the drawing-room, for the professor went straight to his study until dinner and went back again once the meal was finished, excusing himself on the grounds of some case-notes he wished to study.

So Trixie sat with Gumbie, making great play with her needle and thinking about Krijn. She was on the point of going to bed when he came in and sat down. She put down her work in the hope that he wanted to talk but his eye had lighted on the roses which she had put in a corner of the room, out of the way of her carefully arranged vases. She caught his look, and, anxious to please, observed, 'I brought them in here out of the way,' and was rewarded by a growl which could have meant anything and which annoyed her so that she added tartly, 'I couldn't bear to throw them away...'

That was a silly thing to say, she reflected. His, 'Naturally not,' was uttered in a voice of such coldness that she stabbed her needle quite viciously into her work, bundled it up anyhow, and bade him goodnight.

He got up to open the door for her; temper or no temper, his good manners were as natural to him as breathing. She thanked him sweetly and sailed across the hall and upstairs, aware that he was standing in the doorway watching her. Perhaps that made her nervous for she stumbled and fell in an untidy heap before she was halfway up the staircase. He was there, picking her up with the careless ease he might have used for a child, setting her back on her feet with a courteous disinterest. She might indeed have been a child fallen in the street outside, or an old lady needing a helping hand. She felt the childish tears crowding into her throat and without a word flew up the rest of the staircase and into her room where she sat down on her bed and cried her eyes out.

He had left the house when she got down the next morning and Mies told her that he had left a message to say that he would be home in the late afternoon and if he was needed he would be at his rooms.

'Well,' said Trixie brightly, 'how splendid; that means we have the whole day to get everything ready. I'll have my lunch on a tray—an omelette will do. Is everything going well? Do you need anything more? I can go to the shops...'

However, everything was going smoothly; she spent the morning checking all the details, anxious that there should be no hitch that evening, and after her lunch went to her room to put her dress ready for the evening. Olive-green velvet with long tight sleeves and a cream silk waterfall of a collar falling in soft revers, and she would wear the high-heeled slippers which went with it. She went back downstairs; it was almost four o'clock but she thought she would wait for a little in case Krijn got back so that they could have tea together. By half-past four there was no sign of him. She had her own tea and went upstairs to dress, warning Mies to give the professor tea if he wanted it when he returned. He still wasn't back when she got downstairs again and it was now going on for six o'clock and the guests had been asked for seven.

She rang his rooms and caught Mrs Grey as she was on the point of leaving.

'The professor left here just after four o'clock—he was going to see the pathologist at Timothy's about a patient. Would you like me to try and get him for you, Mrs van der Brink-Schaaksma?'

'No, no, don't do that, it might be something important. There's still plenty of time. You're coming, aren't you, Mrs Grey?'

'I'm looking forward to it. I'll give you my phone number at home, shall I? Just on the chance that he doesn't turn up. You could let me know and I'll see if I can find him. He might have gone to a ward.'

Trixie thanked her and put down the receiver. She looked at the clock again and wandered round the house, fidgeting with things and shaking up the cushions which were quite all right as they were. Then she went to the kitchen to be consoled by Mies's comfortable, 'He's a quick dresser, *mevrouw*; give him ten minutes and he'll be looking as though he has done not a thing all day.'

She was quite right; he got home twenty minutes before the first guest arrived and greeted her, freshly shaved and showered, immaculate in one of his dark grey suits, looking as though he had never done a day's work in his life. There was a steady stream of people after that and Trixie, moving around the room, exchanging the kind of talk expected of her, saw little of him. He was a good host; there were no solitary souls shyly propping up the walls or trying to look as though they belonged to a group of people they hardly knew. The shy ones were introduced, then mingled nicely with everyone else, filtered in with a word here and a word there.

No wonder, reflected Trixie, watching him whenever she had the chance, he had been so sought after. She was a good hostess herself; years of helping out at Aunt Alice's social occasions had been an excellent training. The party was a success; the food was just right and the drinks were lavish, and Gladys and her helpers were very good at their jobs. Trixie, listening with that air of interest which so endeared her to those talking to her, glanced around her and was satisfied.

No one hurried away; the party went on for a good deal longer than they had expected, and it was nine o'clock before they sat down to dinner in the little sitting-room. She had prudently decided on a casserole—something which wouldn't spoil and needed the smallest attention from Mies, and its delicious aroma set her small nose quivering.

'It's casserole, I'm afraid,' she observed as they sat down. 'You see it doesn't need much attention and Mies has been so busy...'

'It smells delightful—those appetising bits and pieces looked tempting, but I have always found that at one's own party one never gets around to eating any of them. I'm hungry.'

She beamed at him. 'I'm so glad—so am I. Was the party all right? Are you pleased?'

'I think it was most successful. I must thank you for your efforts.' His eyes rested on her briefly and although he spoke kindly she sensed the coolness. He was still annoyed. You would think, she mused silently, that after three days he would have forgotten about it. She would have to write to Andre and tell him not to send any more flowers. She ate her casserole but no longer with an appetite.

In two days' time it would be Christmas Eve. She spent the rest of the evening making lists of things still to be done, sitting at the table after Gladys had cleared it. Krijn had gone to his study with the request that he shouldn't be disturbed, and wishing her a placid goodnight as he went, and since it would get her nowhere to sit and think about him she soon busied herself with the last-minute details. There were still a few presents to be packed up: the dressing-gown for Mies, and the bag for Gladys; envelopes to be written for the Christmas boxes; flowers to be sent to Matron in both their names. While she was there she might as well write to Andre.

It was a stiff little note, thanking him for the flowers and suggesting that he must have any number of girlfriends who would be delighted to receive such gifts, 'for,' she ended, 'they are wasted on a happily married woman.' She read it through, rather pleased with it, addressed it and took the envelope through to the hall and left it on the console table, ready to post in the morning. He should get it before they got back to Holland. Pleased with herself for writing such a tactful letter, she took herself off to bed. Tomorrow she would go shopping for last-minute odds and ends and hopefully she and Krijn would be friends again. She had quite forgotten the letter in the hall.

Two hours later it caught the professor's eye on his way to bed. He picked it up and studied Trixie's handwriting for a long minute and then put it back on the tray. Presently he went up the staircase, his face an expressionless mask; all the same anyone coming face to face with him then and seeing the blazing rage in his eyes would have been wise to beat a retreat.

Only when he reached his room did Krijn, standing by his open window looking out on to the winter night, observe in a quiet voice, 'I have been a fool—and blind with it.'

At breakfast he behaved as he always did, commenting upon the weather, the party, the Christmas cards they were receiving, and, finally, his doubts as to whether he would be back before the evening.

Trixie, her eyes on his face, murmured suitable replies and he thought savagely that she looked like a child, sitting there, staring at him. She was a child compared with him; he should have thought of that when he had decided to marry her. She might be a levelheaded girl capable of organising life around him so that it didn't interfere with his work and his writing but he had overlooked the fact that she was young—so very much younger than he. Of course it was inevitable that she would respond to a younger man's attentions. He wished suddenly to go to the nearest florist and buy up a shopful of flowers and give them all to her, only if he did that she would think that he was trying to outdo Andre.

He bade her goodbye, expressing the hope that she would enjoy her day, and took himself off to Timothy's where all those who came into contact with him agreed that he had never been so absent-minded. 'It must be that book of his,' commented Sister Snell after he had wandered in and out of the ward several times. 'He is so brilliantly clever but I don't suppose he ever thinks of anything else.'

She was wrong, of course. She was quite wrong! He was thinking of Beatrice.

She was bustling around the house, redoing the flowers, arranging their Christmas cards on one wall of the sitting-room, and putting out fresh candles, and when that was done she got into her outdoor things and took herself off to buy the last-minute things that Mies needed, and since it was Christmas she bought quite a few things that weren't needed and then took herself off to have coffee. There was still a lot of the morning left. She went to St Martin-in-the-Fields, and sat for some time studying the crib and the Christmas tree, uttering wordless prayers and then stuffing almost all the money she had with her into the appeal-for-the-homeless box.

Back at home, she picked at her lunch, something which worried the goodhearted Mies, and then she settled down to an afternoon of tapestry work, interrupted before long by the unexpected arrival of several of the girls she had been friendly with at Timothy's.

'You don't mind?' they wanted to know. 'But we were off duty and someone suggested that we should come and see you.' Jill, plump and easygoing, beamed at her. 'There wasn't much chance to talk to you properly at the ball and we're all dying to know how you are getting on.'

She admired Trixie's elegance and added, 'I must say you look quite different...'

'Well, I'm not,' said Trixie, 'and it's lovely to see you all. We'll have tea presently, but first we'll go round the house if you would like that.'

They had tea round the fire: muffins and fruitcake and little chocolate cakes and all the tea that they could drink, all talking at once about the lovely house. Jill said without envy, 'It must be heavenly to be married to the professor—what wouldn't I give to have someone like him fall in love with me and sweep me off my feet! You looked quite perfect dancing together.'

Trixie said hastily, 'It was a lovely ball, wasn't it? And everyone looked so nice. I liked that dress you were wearing, Jill...'

'I hired it.' There was a chorus of giggles. 'When do you go back to Holland, Trixie?' someone asked—a change in the talk which she welcomed.

They trooped away after tea with a chorus of good wishes and the hopes of seeing her again soon. 'Though I suppose you'll be going to Vienna with the professor, won't you?' asked Jill as they said goodbye. 'He won't want to leave you behind even for a few days.'

That evening Trixie told him of her friends' visit as they sat waiting for dinner, and then said boldly, 'Jill told me that you were going to Vienna; when will that be?'

'Towards the end of January—an international conference.'

'Am I—that is, will you take me with you?'

He spoke pleasantly. 'In the circumstances, I think you might prefer to remain at Schaakslot, with my family.'

'What circumstances?'

'My dear Beatrice, do we need to go into that?'

It was a pity that Gladys came in at that moment to tell them dinner was ready, and during the meal she was given no chance to pursue the matter. They had their coffee at the table and the professor excused himself with the plea of notes to write up.

'Haven't you finished the book yet?' asked Trixie crossly, abandoning her role of compliant wife.

He answered her casually so that she felt even crosser. 'Very soon now. Then we must discuss the situation, must we not?'

'Whatever do you mean?' but he had gone.

'I shall be home for tea,' he told her at breakfast the next day, 'and although I'm going into Timothy's on Christmas Day I shall be free on Boxing Day.'

Her ill humour quite forgotten, Trixie said, 'Oh, splendid! What shall we do?'

He collected up his letters, preparatory to leaving. 'Shall we go to the sea and have that lunch at the Ship Inn? I've booked a table at the Ritz for dinner in the evening.'

Her ordinary little face was transformed with pleasure. 'Oh, Krijn, how lovely, and you will be back for tea?'

'Yes. Do you want to go to the midnight service?'

'Oh, yes, please.' Her smile lighted up the whole of her face. 'What a lovely Christmas we are going to have.'

He didn't answer that, only touched her lightly on the shoulder as he left the room. They had both been out of temper on the previous evening, she reflected, but now everything was all right again. It seemed as though it was; they had tea round the fire with Caesar sitting contentedly between them and later, when Krijn had taken the little dog for a walk, they dined and then sat in companionable silence while he read the paper and she stitched and watched television. Just like an old married couple, thought Trixie, and heaved an unconscious sigh which didn't escape Krijn's hooded eyes.

They went to the church where they had been married; she hadn't suggested it and he had said nothing but she felt no surprise when he parked the car in the rather shabby street and they joined the people streaming in. When they got back home again they wished each other goodnight and since it was past midnight by now he bent to kiss her cheek and wish her a happy Christmas.

'You too, Krijn,' she whispered. She didn't look at him but ran up the staircase. She longed with her whole being to turn round and run back to him, but she didn't.

There were some packages beside her plate in the morning when she got down to breakfast, but before she opened them she gave him her present and watched rather anxiously while he opened it. His 'Just what I can use each day,' was exactly what she had hoped to hear. 'I'm so glad, it's awfully hard to find something for someone like you.' Her eyes lighted on several other parcels beside her plate. 'I wonder who they're all from?'

'We can look and see.'

Mies had given her a pair of knitted gloves and Gladys's packet held fine handkerchiefs. There was a brooch—a lovely mid-Victorian gold circle set with turquoise—from her in-laws, and a long slim case wrapped in gold paper and tied with red ribbon. The case was dark red velvet and inside it was a necklace, a delicate thing of gold entwined with golden leaves and sapphire flowers with pearl centres.

'Oh, my goodness,' breathed Trixie. 'It's from you, Krijn? It's so lovely...' She touched it with a gentle finger. 'I never expected...that is, it's...' She stopped just in time and swallowed back tears.

'It's just right for you, Beatrice,' he finished for her, 'and I am glad that you like it.'

She smiled in a wobbly fashion. 'I'll wear it to the Ritz.'

They went to go to the hospital at midday, when Krijn, having carved the festive bird, took her with him on a tour of the wards. It took some time, for she talked to her friends while he spoke to the patients and exchanged polite greetings with the ward sisters. In Sister Snell's ward, he took her arm for a moment, and she was glad of that, aware that she was being inspected with dislike. She was wearing her wedding outfit and Sister Snell inspected every inch of it while they made polite conversation.

It was pleasant to be home again and have their tea and then, later, their Christmas dinner, a meal which Mies had cooked to perfection. It had been a lovely day, thought Trixie, curled up in her bed later, and she got out of it to take another look at the necklace. It was such a lovely thing and she was thrilled with it. She would have been even more thrilled, she thought wistfully, if it had been given with love.

Even if the professor had no love to give her, he had friendship. Boxing Day was a great success; they drove to the east coast and walked where they had walked before and had a snack lunch at the Ship Inn, and that evening they dined and danced at the Ritz. She wore the necklace and the earrings and because she was with Krijn, dancing in his arms, she was happy. Only later, thinking about the day, came the thought that not once had their talk been about anything that mattered. When he wasn't wrapped in one of his spells of absent-mindedness, Krijn was adept at what she called social talk, and that was all that had passed between them all day. She might have been a casual acquaintance, a seldom-met member of the family, even a patient.

CHAPTER NINE

NOTHING had been planned for the day after Boxing Day. The professor had done his final round at Timothy's and seen his last private patients and he wouldn't be returning until the end of February unless he was needed for consultations. The day would be free, thought Trixie as she got out of bed; the packing wouldn't take more than half an hour or so, and she would have to have a talk with Mies, but otherwise the day was theirs. She wondered what they would do with it—a day out perhaps? A drive into the country? She went down to breakfast full of expectation.

Over that meal Krijn observed, 'Did I tell you that there will be several people coming in for coffee this morning?'

Trixie put down her cup with rather an unsteady hand. 'No, you didn't. Have you any idea how many?'

He looked vague. 'Oh, people from Timothy's to wish us *bon voyage*.'

'I see. And will there be people coming to tea as well?'

'Oh, very likely...'

'Well, I'll mention it to Mies. We can't go out.'

He shot her a sudden sharp glance. 'Did you want to?'

'Not in the least, I have any number of things to do before we leave.'

She went to see Mies after breakfast, arranged for there to be a steady flow of coffee and biscuits if they were needed, warned her that there might be people for tea as well and then settled down to a talk about the running of the house while they were away. The professor had been in the habit of paying a cheque into the bank each month to cover household expenses and the wages while he was absent. 'More than enough,' said Mies in her awkward English, 'but now I am able to send the receipts to you? Then it is not necessary to bother the professor.'

'Yes, do that, Mies, and if you want any more money or there is anything worrying you then let me know. It might save bothering the professor.'

She went to her room then and made sure that her hair and face were fit for visitors; luckily she had put on a pretty blue cashmere top and a matching corduroy skirt that morning, quite suitable for morning coffee. She added the gold chain just to be festive and went to join Krijn in the drawing-room. Just in time; it seemed almost all his colleagues and their wives were bent on coming to wish them a happy New Year in Holland. Trixie, dispensing coffee and small talk, marvelled at the number of friends Krijn had. Since it was the festive season most of them were on their way to visit family or friends so that by midday they were on their own again.

'I'll take Caesar for a walk,' said the professor, and wandered away without asking her if she would like to go with them. She went and finished her packing and joined him for lunch, determinedly cheerful.

There were more visitors for tea and when the last of them had gone Krijn went to his study to clear his desk and although they dined amicably enough he didn't stay more than half an hour in the drawing-room with her, going back to his study with the plea that he wished to correct the first chapters of his book and return them before they left England. After breakfast the next morning he got into his car and took them to his publisher, returning just in time for an early lunch before they were to drive down to Dover.

It was hard to leave Mies and Gladys and even harder to say goodbye to Caesar. 'If you made Holland your real home,' said Trixie in the car, 'you could take Caesar there. Couldn't you just pop over here for a day or two from time to time? I know you do that now, but I mean just for a day or two. Mies and Gladys could come too, couldn't they?'

'That is, of course, possible,' he conceded, 'but when I was unmarried I had no strong urge or reason to have a permanent home.'

'But you are married now,' Trixie pointed out in a matter-of-fact voice, and added uncertainly, 'Don't you want to settle down?'

'Yes, I do, but circumstances may not permit that.' His tone was dismissive and when she peered sideways at him his mouth was set so grimly that she prudently forbore from asking any more questions. All the same, she spent almost all of the journey to Dover wondering what those circumstances might be.

It had turned very cold and the afternoon was already darkening. It was quite dark when they landed and began the long drive up to Holland, and when they were almost at Leiden it began to snow.

'Good,' said Krijn idly. 'Perhaps we shall get some skating this winter.' He glanced at her. 'Do you skate, Beatrice?'

'No, but I dare say I could learn...'

'There will be plenty of people ready to teach you.' He sounded uninterested and he didn't speak again until they came to a smooth halt before their own massive door.

It was flung open at once by Rabo, with Wolke standing beside him and Samson prancing up and down on the steps uttering little yelps of pleasure. He reared up on his hind legs to greet them in turn and Trixie said happily, 'Oh, it's good to be home,' and then shook hands with Wolke and Rabo, not seeing the faint frown on Krijn's face.

The old house welcomed them with its soft lights and warmth and when they went into the drawing-room there was Percy, sitting where he always sat, rousing himself sufficiently to murmur at them before curling up once more.

It was late by now but Wolke had supper for them, set out on a small table in the small sitting-room, and she trotted to and fro with soup and a soufflé, creamed spinach and a dish of *poffertjes* while Rabo fetched in their cases. All the while she talked; Trixie, struggling to understand, gathered that all had gone well while they had been away and that everything was ready for the New Year.

'When does everyone come?' asked Trixie of Krijn.

'In two days' time. Wolke will want to talk to you about the arrangements; perhaps you can find the time tomorrow—Rabo will be there to translate.'

'Yes, of course. But won't you be at home?'

'I've several appointments tomorrow, both at the hospital and at my rooms as well as an outpatients' clinic. I'm sure you will have plenty to keep you busy. You may have visitors—the family know that we are back.'

'Oh, good. Will you be back before tea?'

'Very unlikely.' He glanced at his watch. 'It is very late—are you not tired?'

She thought that she was boring him, although he was far too well mannered to let it show. She got to her feet at once, almost knocking over her chair in her haste. 'Yes, I am. I'll go to bed. Goodnight, Krijn.' She whisked herself out of the room without looking at him. To smile would have been impossible and it would never do to let him see the silly tears she was determined not to shed.

He had gone in the morning; she breakfasted alone with Percy for company and spent the morning sitting at the kitchen table with Wolke, armed with lists and paper and pencil and with Rabo there, carefully translating for them both, and just now and again Trixie managed a word or two in Dutch which gave them all satisfaction. Refreshments were discussed, meals mulled over, the question of extra help talked about, and would Mevrouw see to the flower arrangements? It was evident that Rabo and Wolke knew exactly what to do and could indeed have managed very well without her; after all, Krijn had been leaving it to them to arrange for a good many years. She beamed at them, awfully grateful that they had accepted her so wholeheartedly. Then she went away to make her own lists and presently drove carefully to Leiden to buy the flowers.

It was very satisfying to be able to choose the flowers she wanted without thinking of the cost. There were jonquils and lilac, tulips in abundance and freesias and hyacinths. She loaded the back of the Mini and went back to spend the rest of the day arranging them. She was filling a small crystal vase with lily-of-the-valley and grape hyacinths to put on Krijn's desk when Andre said from the door, 'What a charming picture, and how delightful it is to see you again, Beatrice.'

She turned to look at him, annoyance battling with good manners.

'Hello, Andre. I am very busy. Did you want to see Krijn?'

'No. I came to see you.'

'Well, I'm sorry but I really can't spare the time to chat. You'll be here for New Year, won't you?'

'Oh, yes—there will be the entire family here, but there won't be a chance to get you alone.'

'But I don't want to be alone with you, Andre.' Trixie sounded coolly matter-of-fact. She cast him a cold look. 'I think you must be a very conceited man and I wish you would go away.'

When he laughed and didn't move she picked up the vase, carried it to the study, and, back in the hall, said, 'I'm going to help Wolke in the kitchen. I'm sorry I can't offer you tea.' She gave him a tolerant smile. 'Goodbye, Andre.'

The professor had got through his day rather more quickly than he had expected. He made short work of the notes for the various doctors whose patients he had seen, handed them over to Juffrouw Niep to type and got into his car. Tea in the drawing-room with Beatrice sitting opposite him, lamplight shining on her neat mousy head, listening to his day's work, looking up from time to time and smiling. She had a lovely smile and her eyes sparkled; he had never thought of her as pretty but now, with all the clarity of a man suddenly in love, he knew that she was beautiful. He drove home a little too fast and only slowed as he reached his gates. He was on the sweep before the house when he saw the other car parked before the door and recognised it as Andre's. He sat looking at it, the engine idling, and then he turned and drove back the way he had come, out of the drive and into the lane, back to Leiden and from there to the coast, to Katwijk-aan-Zee, where he parked the car and got out and walked along the promenade in the teeth of a cruelly cold wind, bringing with it the beginnings of the snow which had been threatening. He walked for an hour or more and then got back into the car and drove himself home once more.

The car had gone; he parked the Bentley in the garage and went in through the kitchen door where Trixie was sitting at the kitchen table stuffing olives while Wolke stood at the stove, stirring something which smelled delicious. Trixie saw him first and jumped up. 'Krijn—I thought you said you'd be home for tea.' She saw his wet coat and the bleakness of his face. 'Has something happened? You're so wet—let me have that coat and Wolke will warm some coffee. We can have dinner earlier if you would like that.'

He tossed his coat on to a chair and pulled Samson's ears gently. 'No need, but coffee would be welcome. Perhaps I might have it in my study? There is some phoning I must do.'

When the coffee was ready Trixie picked up the tray and went along to the study. The professor was sitting with the great dog beside him. There was a pile of papers before him but he wasn't looking at them.

'Krijn, what's worrying you, what's wrong? Are you all right?'

He smiled a little. 'I've had a heavy day. I'll just do the telephoning, then go and change.' He glanced at his watch. 'I've half an hour, at least, haven't I?' Whatever it was, she wasn't to be told. She went quietly from the room and back to the kitchen and then presently upstairs to shower and change into one of her pretty dresses.

It was during dinner that the professor asked casually, 'Have you had a pleasant day, Beatrice?'

'Oh, yes. I talked to Wolke and bought the flowers and spent the afternoon arranging them.' She hesitated. 'This afternoon Andre called...'

'Oh!' He sounded only vaguely interested. 'Can't he come for New Year?'

'Yes, he's coming. I—I don't know why he came...'

'To see you, perhaps?'

Trixie blushed and looked guilty, which was a pity since she had no reason to be. It was a pity, too, that she couldn't think of the right answer to that. The professor watched her tell-tale face and sighed gently. He had never, after all, allowed her to be more than a friend; he couldn't blame her for falling in love with a man, so much younger than he, who sent her roses and wrote her letters. He was entirely to blame; he had married her because it suited him to take a wife and he was being paid back in his own coin. He said mildly, 'Is everything arranged for New Year?'

She answered him eagerly, glad to change the conversation. 'Yes. I think it's just as you like it to be...' She went into rather too much detail about the plans and he listened with every appearance of interest while he watched her face. Why, he wondered, had he not seen how gentle her mouth was, how sweetly she smiled, what pretty hands she had? His smile was faint and derogatory; he was behaving like a lovesick youth.

He sat in the drawing-room with her after dinner, keeping up a steady flow of small talk about his family and their arrival the next day.

'I'll have go to Leiden in the morning, but I'll be back in good time for lunch. Mother and Father will be here and possibly Luisje and Alco. The rest of them should be here by teatime.'

'I'm looking forward to it. I hope everything will go exactly right...'

'I can't imagine why it shouldn't.'

She went up to bed presently, excited and a little apprehensive about a house full of guests, and she stayed awake for a long while, wondering what had made Krijn look so strange when he had come home. He had said that he was tired but even after only a few weeks of marriage she knew him well enough to know that he wasn't a man to tire easily. A hard day's work and getting caught in bad weather was something he would toss off without a thought. Why had he been so wet anyway? He had been in the car, hadn't he? His coat had been soaking; a thick jacket, heavily lined, which would take an hour's downpour to reduce it to such a terrible state... there was something wrong.

He was his usual calm self when he got back the next morning. His parents had already arrived and so had Luisje and Alco as well as Pibbe and Bruno and the twins. Lunch was a lively meal, and shortly afterwards Soeske and Reka joined them with their husbands and children. The house came alive with the children running to and fro and the grown-ups catching up on all the family news. Trixie found herself drawn into their circle, being questioned about their Christmas in London, listening to snippets of gossip. She discovered that she was enjoying herself despite the fact that Krijn and she had very little opportunity to be together. The children took a great deal of his attention and the men tended to gather together and talk, and when he did speak to her she sensed his coldness despite his pleasant manner. There were so many people there, she consoled herself, it would go unnoticed. Only it didn't; her mother-in-law's eyes had seen through her son's bland manner towards his wife, and she wondered about it.

After tea everyone dispersed to dress for the evening. Trixie had decided to wear the green velvet—it seemed to her to be the most suitable for her role of hostess—and she put on the necklace and the earrings too and they were remarked upon when they all gathered once more, this time without the children, before dinner. 'Krijn gave you them, of course,' observed her mother-in-law, and Trixie touched the necklace with a gentle finger.

'Yes, isn't it lovely—the earrings too.'

She had gone to great pains over the dinner and the dining table, the silverware and crystal sparkled on the damask cloth and the centre-piece of holly and Christmas roses and blue hyacinths had taken her a long time to do, and the food, chosen with such care with Wolke, was very delicious: cold watercress soup, roast goose, champagne sorbets, and a magnificent trifle. Over the cheese and biscuits everyone praised the meal and Soeske said, 'Krijn, you have a wonderful little wife...'

'Yes, I know...' He raised his glass to Trixie, sitting at the other end of the table, and someone cried 'speech' but he shook his head. 'The guests we have coming will be arriving at any moment now—we had better go into the drawing-room.'

Krijn had a great number of friends and family and they all came. The rooms filled with laughing, chattering groups, drinking champagne and nibbling the canapés Trixie and Wolke had agreed upon, and presently someone turned on a cassette and everyone took to the floor. Trixie, circling the drawing-room with Krijn, saw Andre first. He had just arrived and was talking to Luisje while his eyes roamed the room and fastened on Trixie, who looked away quickly with a brief smile.

'This is a lovely way to see the New Year in,' she observed to Krijn a little too brightly, and he, who had seen Andre at the same time as she had and noted the smile, agreed in a silky voice which she found disturbing.

After that dance she gaily changed from partner to partner, contriving to keep away from Andre. Not for long, however; she couldn't avoid him all evening.

'I want to talk to you,' he said softly. 'Can we not escape somewhere quiet?'

'Certainly not, and anyway I don't want to.' She added crisply, 'I wish you would find yourself a girl, Andre. Do you like making mischief?'

He gave a little crow of laughter. 'Ah—has my sleepy-eyed cousin woken up at last? It will do him good to discover that life isn't always exactly as he intends it to be.'

'I don't understand you,' said Trixie in a stony voice, 'and if we were anywhere else I would slap your face for that. Krijn is a wonderful man and the finest husband in the world.'

'I do believe you're in love with him.' Andre sounded uncertain.

'Of course I am; why else would I marry him? And now you must excuse me—I want to speak to my mother-in-law.'

She slipped away to join that lady sitting in a quiet corner and sat down beside her. Mevrouw van der Brink-Schaaksma saw her eyes sparkling with rage and the colour in her cheeks and looked round for her son. He was dancing with an elderly cousin who lived at the other end of the country and rarely met the family. He was listening with every appearance of interest to what she was telling him, but behind his placid face his mother knew that he was holding down a rage as strong as Trixie's. She said cheerfully, 'I saw you dancing with Andre. He's family so of course he gets invited to all the family gatherings, but he isn't like the rest of us; he adores making mischief—it's high time he settled down. I do hope that he will meet some strong-minded woman who will change his ways for him.'

'You won't mind if I say that I don't like him? He's amusing but he's unkind too...'

Her mother-in-law patted her knee. 'I don't like him either,' she said comfortably. 'How nice you look, dear, you have excellent taste. Krijn is proud of you.'

Trixie said softly, 'I'm proud of him too.' She smiled at her companion. 'I'd better just make sure Rabo has everything ready—it's almost midnight.'

Someone switched off the music and turned on the radio while the champagne was carried round and Rabo, Wolke and the two maids with glasses in their hands took their places by the door as the first stroke of the New Year sounded. Trixie, standing with Krijn, drank her champagne and said shyly, 'Happy New Year, Krijn.'

'Happy New Year to you, Beatrice.' He caught her close and kissed her hard. She had closed her own eyes and when she opened them she saw that his were hard and cold like steel. How is it possible, she thought in bewilderment, to kiss that way and look like that at the same time? She had no chance to think any more about it; everyone was moving round the room, greeting everyone else, and when she came face to face with Andre she turned her face so that his kiss hardly brushed her cheek.

It was two o'clock before the last guest had gone and the family had wished each other a sleepy goodnight and gone to their beds. Trixie lay awake for a long time, listening to the comforting creaks and rustles of the old house as it settled into the quiet of the night while she tried to think sensibly about Krijn and herself. He was angry; she knew him well enough to know that, but she didn't think he was angry with her—and besides he had kissed her in a most satisfactory manner. Dwelling upon the delightful memory she fell asleep.

It seemed, in the light of early morning, the sensible thing to do was to have a talk to Krijn. Everyone would be leaving some time during the day but perhaps in the evening...

She hardly saw him to speak to during that day; she was fully occupied with her duties as hostess, and when at last they had waved away the final carload Krijn observed that he had a good deal of telephone calls to make and would be in his study until dinner. So Trixie took a long time changing into her prettiest dress, did her face and hair, taking pains over them both, wound the gold chain round her neck and went to the drawing-room where she arranged herself under the pink-shaded lamp and took up her needlework, aware that she looked rather nice in its dim light and anxious to make a good impression when Krijn joined her. 'I am no beauty,' she confided to Percy, sitting curled up at her feet, 'but I am fast learning to make the most of what I have.'

She mulled over what she was going to say and since she had to make up Krijn's answers she was fairly satisfied with the result. It was a pity that when he did come he said almost at once, 'I should really go to the hospital after dinner—you don't mind?'

The neat arrangement of questions and answers she had rehearsed so carefully was shattered. She said with unwonted tartness, 'Yes, I do mind. You're only going so that you don't have to spend the evening here with me.' She glared at him so fiercely that he smiled, which spurred her on to utter a hotchpotch of muddled thoughts, which, while not making sense, allowed him to see that she was in a splendid rage. 'And I want to know,' she finished, 'why you are so angry about something. What have I done?'

His calm was infuriating. 'You have done nothing; indeed I am not angry with you, Beatrice. Angry at myself, yes, and circumstances... I should not have married you, you know—I did it for my own convenience, you understood that, did you not? But I failed to take into account that you are so much younger than I. It is only natural that you should find in Andre all the things lacking in me.'

'Are you saying that you wouldn't mind...that is, if...' She faltered, horrified at what she was going to say.

The professor had strolled to the window and was standing with his back to her, looking out into the dark garden. 'I would like you to be happy, Beatrice.'

'You would let me go?' she asked quietly.

'Oh, yes, if you wished—I should miss you, but I have my work.' It seemed to her that he sounded both impatient and a little bored.

'Your work's very important to you, isn't it?'

'Yes. Now, having cleared the air, shall we have a drink before dinner?'

She sipped her sherry. For her the air wasn't clear at all; she was in a fog of misunderstanding and she wasn't sure what to do next. He was a kind man, often lost in thought, absorbed in his work, frequently oblivious to what was going on around him but now he had got this idea in his head about Andre and it seemed to her that he didn't mind. Perhaps he wished that he had never married her? In which case, she would only make things worse by telling him that she loved him, something she very much wanted to do. But she held her tongue.

They dined in a civilised manner, talking trivialities while she reflected that if only she could see beyond that bland face sitting opposite to her, and shout and rave and have a good cry, they might be able to understand each other.

Indeed, she was on the point of that when Rabo came in to say that Mijnheer ter Vange was on the phone and would Mevrouw care to drive up to Alkmaar on the following afternoon? He had business there and she might enjoy the run.

'I shall be delighted,' said Trixie without stopping to think. If Krijn wanted to get rid of her, she would do all she could to assist him. She peeped at him over the floral arrangement in the centre of the table but there was nothing to see in his face. 'I shall enjoy it,' she added defiantly and rather too loudly, hoping that he might say something—anything. However, he didn't.

She went to bed early and cried herself to sleep. Of course she wouldn't spend the afternoon with Andre— any man with sense would have guessed that, but Krijn, engrossed in his horrible glands, had forgotten about women and falling in love and being misunderstood. She woke several times during the night and snivelled in a miserable way so that when she got down to breakfast she looked just about as plain as a girl could look. Not that he'll notice, she told her reflection as she piled her hair untidily; he doesn't even see me.

She was wrong, of course—the professor noted every small detail as she sat down at the table and wished him a cool good morning and presently he asked, 'At what time is Andre coming for you?'

She crumbled toast, not looking at him. 'I suppose after lunch.' She drew a steadying breath. 'Krijn...'

He was already on his feet, and halfway to the door he paused long enough to tell her that he didn't expect to be home until the evening. 'Enjoy your day,' he told her.

Trixie, a mild-tempered girl, sat and seethed. He wasn't going to give her a chance to say anything, and, anyway, how would she say it? Meet him in the hall when he got home and tell him that she loved him and what did he intend to do about it? 'That is the last thing I shall do,' she told Percy, drowsing under the table.

She planned her day carefully. Andre knew that they lunched normally at half-past twelve, so he wouldn't arrive until after that. She asked Wolke if she might have a light lunch at noon sharp, discussed the evening's meal with her, approved some necessary purchases, rearranged the flowers and went to look at the weather. The sky was grey and lowering and faintly yellow round the edges. There had been a frost overnight and the shrubs and trees were weighed down with ice; moreover, Rabo, bringing in the coffee-tray, informed her in his atrocious English that the weather was worsening. 'Not a day in which to travel, *mevrouw*. There will be bad weather very soon.'

She ate her lunch quickly and went to her room, where she pulled on boots, dragged a woolly cap down over her ears and got into her parka. A walk would clear her head and there was a good deal of open country to the north of the village between the motorways going to Amsterdam. She would take a closer look at the lake; an hour's brisk walk would get her to it... She had her hand on the door when Rabo appeared from nowhere to enquire if she would be back shortly. 'I think you go out with Mijnheer ter Vange?' he said.

'Well, no—I've changed my mind. Will you tell him when he comes, please?'

'Certainly, *mevrouw*. You will be back for tea?'

'I don't know...'

'If I may speak, *mevrouw*, the weather will be bad very soon now.'

'I'll take shelter, Rabo, don't worry about me. I feel like a good walk.'

She set off briskly, glad to be out of doors even though it was already getting dark and the wind from the sea was icy. The road was a lonely one running between polder land and empty save for a farmhouse or two in the distance. She hardly noticed that; indeed, she didn't notice where she was going until she saw a glimmer of water a short distance from the brick road she was on.

It glinted like cold steel under the darkening sky and just for a moment she hesitated, but she had come quite a long way by now and to go back without actually getting a close view of the lake seemed silly. She slid down the dyke upon which the road was built and started walking towards the water. Until that moment she hadn't paid heed to the unnatural darkness, nor had she noticed that the wind had dropped. She stopped, suddenly uneasy, and looked behind her. Grey fog was rolling in from the sea, blanketing the open country; she was halfway back to the road when it enveloped her in icy swirls so that she could no longer see. She stood still, dumb with fright, wondering what to do. The fog was ice-cold, and she would freeze to death if she stood still, but on the other hand she didn't dare to move. The unpleasant thought that people lost in fog walked round in circles crossed her mind. 'Krijn—Krijn, do come.' The ridiculous words, uttered in a wispy voice, were carried away by the soft gloom swirling round her. 'He can't hear,' she added, taking comfort from the sound of her voice. It was a cold comfort.

The professor wasn't able to hear her, but he was thinking about her. He had had a heavy morning; a ward-round, his clinic in Outpatients and then his private patients, whom he had seen in his rooms and the last of whom had just left. Juffrouw Niep had gone to her lunch and he sat at his desk, a cooling cup of coffee before him and the faithful Samson's bulk squashed around his feet. Beatrice's unhappy face was vivid in his mind—she had wanted to say something to him at breakfast and he hadn't stayed to listen. He glanced at his watch; even now she was probably getting into Andre's car, a bit early perhaps. If he went home now he might be able to persuade her not to go, at least until they had talked. He was, he told himself, quite prepared to listen; he was a reasonable man although he had to admit to a strong desire to batter Andre into the ground. His nurse came in with a plate of sandwiches and put it down beside the coffee.

'I have to go home, Zuster,' he told her. 'There is nothing for this afternoon, is there? Ask Juffrouw Niep to make any appointments for tomorrow; I want to be free for the remainder of today. Refer anything urgent to my registrar at the hospital, will you?'

The nurse, rather mystified, went away, and he telephoned the hospital, spoke to his registrar and left his rooms with Samson. Outside the fog was sliding gently into Leiden and he was forced to drive slowly as he left the town behind him. The village was already blanketed and Rabo had turned on the lights at the gate as he turned the car into the drive. He was at the door before the professor had got out of his car, looking as agitated as his unflappable dignity would allow. Normally he spoke Dutch but now he broke into Friese. 'I telephoned the hospital and your rooms, Professor. Mevrouw went out more than an hour ago...'

'With Mijnheer ter Vange?'

'No, no. She wished to go for a walk; she left a message to say that she had changed her mind. He arrived—oh, perhaps half an hour after she had gone. He was most annoyed, he got into his car and drove away; he said he would return to den Haag.'

The professor was getting out of his coat and shrugging on a heavy jacket. 'Which way did she go, Rabo?'

'Not to the village, for I watched her turn away. Perhaps to the lake? She said to Wolke that she would like to walk there one day...'

'Good lord, it's three miles, and not a house or a farm near the dyke road.'

He was putting on thick gloves. 'Keep Samson in, will you? I'll take the torch and the brandy from the car and go after her. The fog's thick here, it will be worse towards the lake. Don't do anything for the moment. She's a sensible girl and won't panic, but if we're not back by six o'clock get a search-party organised.'

He disappeared into the fog and Rabo shut the door and led a reluctant Samson down to the kitchen, where he informed Wolke that the professor was in a fine taking and hadn't she better have everything prepared in case Mevrouw came back soaked to the skin and half dead with cold?

'She shouldn't have gone,' he observed. 'It's my opinion that she didn't want to go out with Mijnheer ter Vange.'

'Well, of course she didn't, hasn't got eyes for anyone but the professor. I'll set a tea-tray ready for when they get back.'

The professor's powerful torch allowed him to see a foot or so before him, and besides he knew the country around him—as long as he kept to the brick road he would be all right. He strode ahead until he saw by the light of his torch that he had walked for half an hour— about halfway to the lake. The fog was dense now and he slowed his steps, remembering the narrow path which was a short cut to the water and one which he had taken many times when he had gone fishing. He stood for a moment and shouted and heard his own voice echoing in the silence, and then he walked on, shouting at intervals, but it wasn't for another twenty minutes or so that he heard a faint answer. He bellowed again and this time he was sure. The path must be very near by now and he spent a few minutes casting round with the torch looking for it and once on it the going became difficult; it was freezing now and the ground was treacherous underfoot. Every few yards he stopped to shout, aware that a fine rage was building up inside him born of the fear he had refused to admit to. He paused once more and shouted in a great voice and then stopped dead when Beatrice said within inches of him, 'You don't need to shout, I'm here...' Her voice was quavery and thick with tears but his strong feelings didn't allow him to notice that.

'What in the name of heaven are you doing out here? You little fool, you could have frozen solid; as it is I dare say you've got pneumonia.' All the same he had put his arms around her and was hugging her close.

She was numb with cold—she would never, she thought, get warm again—and she was grateful for his reassuring bulk, but he had spoken harshly and one or two tears dribbled down her cheeks. She had made a fine mess of things...

'You didn't go with Andre,' observed Krijn. He was rubbing her hands and arms.

'Well, of course I didn't. I never meant to.'

'Stamp your feet, we've quite a long walk home. So why did you accept his invitation when he phoned?'

Her voice was very small. 'I wanted to annoy you.'

He stopped his rubbing and caught her close again. 'Will you tell me why, my darling?' He sighed. 'I thought that you had fallen in love with him.'

'Well, I hadn't.' She took a deep breath, and said through chattering teeth, 'I've fallen in love with you.'

'Ah,' said the professor, and heaved a deep sigh of contentment. Considerably hampered by the grey fog, his kiss was, none the less, deeply satisfying.

'We'll go home now,' he told her. 'It would, in the light of this most interesting discovery, be foolish of us to remain here and freeze to death.'

The way back seemed never-ending. Trixie's legs were numb, she felt as though she were covered in ice despite Krijn's great arms around her, and her mind was numb too. Krijn didn't speak except to give her an encouraging word from time to time and when suddenly, as they were almost home, the fog thinned and rolled away and he turned to look at her, she burst into tears.

He didn't say anything then either, but picked her up and carried her the rest of the way, to be met in the drive by an anxious Rabo.

'Tell Wolke to run a warm bath and make a pot of tea. No harm done, I think, only very cold.'

He carried Trixie, still sniffling and gulping, up the staircase and into her room, handed her over to Wolke and went along to his room with Samson crowding at his heels.

An hour later, nicely warm once more, dressed in a becoming cashmere sweater and skirt, her hair neat and her still pale face nicely made up, Trixie went down to the drawing-room. She peeped round the door but the room was empty and she crossed to the fire and gave a small squeak as Krijn got up from a chair in the window.

'I thought you weren't here,' she said awkwardly. 'I'll just go and see if Wolke needs...'

'Did you mean it?' asked the professor, and something in his voice made her smile slowly.

'Yes, I did, oh, I certainly did, Krijn.'

He had taken her in his arms. 'I thought that I had lost you, that I would have to let you go. You see, I think I have loved you for weeks, but it wasn't until you had those flowers from Andre that I knew. But I do know now, my darling. Might we not start again?'

'Yes, oh, yes, but——'

He kissed her into a rapturous silence. 'I love you, I am absent-minded and forgetful, but I promise you that I shall never forget you...'

'I shan't give you the chance,' said Trixie. She looked up into his face with shining eyes and what she saw there made her very happy. She stood on tiptoe, the better to put her arms around his neck, and kissed him, and Rabo, coming in to say that dinner was served, went away again, to tell Wolke to keep everything hot for the moment.

'It will be ruined—the fricassee—and the asparagus...'

'Don't worry,' said Rabo, and he chuckled. 'They won't notice.'

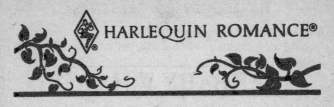

BARBARY WHARF

**An exciting six-book series, one title per month
beginning in October, by bestselling author**

Charlotte Lamb

Set in the glamorous and fast-paced world of international
journalism, BARBARY WHARF will take you from the
Sentinel's hectic newsroom to the most thrilling cities in the
world. You'll meet media tycoon Nick Caspian and his
adversary Gina Tyrrell, whose dramatic story of passion and
heartache develops throughout the six-book series.

In book one, BESIEGED (#1498), you'll also meet Hazel and
Piet. Hazel's always had a good word to say about everyone.
Well, almost. She just can't stand Piet Van Leyden, Nick's
chief architect and one of the most arrogant know-it-alls she's
ever met! As far as Hazel's concerned, Piet's a twentieth-
century warrior, and she's the one being besieged!

Don't miss the sparks in the first BARBARY WHARF
book, BESIEGED (#1498), available in October from
Harlequin Presents.

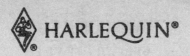

HARLEQUIN®

THE TAGGARTS OF TEXAS!

Harlequin's Ruth Jean Dale brings you
THE TAGGARTS OF TEXAS!

Those Taggart men—strong, sexy and hard to resist...

You've met Jesse James Taggart in FIREWORKS!
Harlequin Romance #3205 (July 1992)

Now meet Trey Smith—he's THE RED-BLOODED YANKEE!
Harlequin Temptation #413 (October 1992)

Then there's Daniel Boone Taggart in SHOWDOWN!
Harlequin Romance #3242 (January 1993)

And finally the Taggarts who started it all—in LEGEND!
Harlequin Historical #168 (April 1993)

Read all the Taggart romances!
Meet all the Taggart men!

Available wherever Harlequin books are sold.

WELCOME TO

The quintessential small town, where everyone
knows everybody else!

**Finally, books that capture the pleasure
of tuning in to your favorite TV show!**

Join your friends at Tyler in the eighth book, BACHELOR'S PUZZLE by Ginger
Chambers, available in October.

*What do Tyler's librarian and a cosmopolitan architect have in common? What
does the coroner's office have to reveal?*

GREAT READING...GREAT SAVINGS...
AND A FABULOUS FREE GIFT!

Each book set in Tyler is a self-contained love story; together, the twelve novels
stitch the fabric of the community. You can't miss the Tyler books on the shelves
because the covers honor the old American tradition of quilting; each cover
depicts a patch of the large Tyler quilt!

And you can receive a FABULOUS GIFT, ABSOLUTELY FREE, by collecting
proofs-of-purchase found in each Tyler book, *and* use our Tyler coupons to save
on your next TYLER book purchase.

Back by Popular Demand

Janet Dailey
Americana

Janet Dailey takes you on a romantic tour of America through fifty favorite Harlequin Presents novels, each one set in a different state and researched by Janet and her husband, Bill.

A journey of a lifetime. The perfect collectible series!

October titles
#41 SOUTH DAKOTA
Dakota Dreaming
#42 TENNESSEE
Sentimental Journey